Sunsphere

Sunsphere

Andrew Farkas

BLAZEVOX[BOOKS]
Buffalo, New York

Sunsphere
by Andrew Farkas
Copyright © 2019

Published by BlazeVOX [books]

All rights reserved. No part of this book may be reproduced without the publisher's written permission, except for brief quotations in reviews.

Printed in the United States of America

Interior design and typesetting by Geoffrey Gatza
Cover Art: Scott Schulman

First Edition
ISBN: 978-1-60964-324-9
Library of Congress Control Number: 2018951447

BlazeVOX [books]
131 Euclid Ave
Kenmore, NY 14217
Editor@blazevox.org

publisher of weird little books

BlazeVOX [books]

blazevox.org

21 20 19 18 17 16 15 14 13 12 01 02 03 04 05 06 07 08 09 10

BlazeVOX

Acknowledgements

The author would like to thank the following journals and presses for publishing sections of this book.

"Do Kids in California Dream of North Carolina?" in *New Orleans Review* 32.2.

"No Tomorrow" in *PANK* 2.

"The Physics of the Bottomless Pit" in *Berkeley Fiction Review* 25.

"Everything Under the Sunsphere" in *Harpur Palate* 5.2[*].

"White Dwarf Blues" in *Northwest Review* 45-2.

"I Don't Know Why" in *Quarter After Eight* 16.

"Zeno's Shotgun Paradox" in *Atticus Review* 1.8.

"The City of the Sunsphere" in *Denver Quarterly* 49.1.

"You Are Where I Am Not" in *The Brooklyn Rail* (June 2009).

---

[*] This selection was nominated for a Pushcart Prize.

for Jim Westlake

Table of Contents

Do Kids in California Dream of North Carolina? 13

The City of the Sunsphere 34

Zeno's Shotgun Paradox 51

The Physics of the Bottomless Pit 61

No Tomorrow 103

Everything Under the Sunsphere 138

White Dwarf Blues 158

I Don't Know Why 189

You Are Where I Am Not 226

Gene.

Yeah.

If you run off from here you'll wind up like Slusser.

You mean with a pick on my leg?

I mean you'll be in and out of institutions for the rest of your life.

Save for one thing.

What's that.

They aint goin to catch me.

Where will you go?

Go to Knoxville.

Knoxville.

Hell yes.

What makes you think they wont find you in Knoxville?

Hell fire Sut. Big a place as Knoxville is? They never would find ye there. Why you wouldnt even know where to start huntin somebody.

Cormac McCarthy
Suttree

Sunsphere

Do Kids in California Dream of North Carolina?

"Heisenberg May Have Slept Here."
- Bumper Sticker

On a television leaning against a floor-to-ceiling window in the southern portion of the peninsular apartment, a late-night talk show host claims, "Scientists no longer believe that the universe will be destroyed by fire. They used to think the whole place was going to burn up one day, but not anymore. Now they say the universe will eventually run out of the energy it needs to keep everything going, that it will just keep expanding and expanding out into complete chaos where everything will break down. So, it's pretty much like Los Angeles." The audience laughs.

Trevor is unable to laugh because he wonders, as he forever works at solving the mystery of his Rubik's Cube, why a late-night show is on during the day. He sits in a chair, facing a set of bookcases perpendicular to the television set. Trevor once believed in mathematics, experimentation, and causality. Now there is only speculation, observation, and probability. Life is uncertain, indeterminate, chaotic. Toys are as likely to hold answers as anything. Yet like Einstein searching for a local hidden variable theory that would restore determinism and causality to measurements, Trevor hopes order will return when he finally solves the Cube. It has to. There's nothing else.

Trevor says: "There must be an energetic center to life. There must be a focal point where it all makes sense," and keeps manipulating the toy.

Kat says: "Ninety million miles is one Astronomical Unit, or AU." She makes campy quotes in the air with her fingers when she says *AU,* and continues shuffling zombie-like in an ellipse of unknown momentum around the coffee table in the center of the room, mumbling numbers, computations, formulae, equations, differentials, smoking a cigarette, ashing on the floor, staring at the debris-covered ground. She does not care what time it is.

Indeed, although the television displays a late-night talk show host performing his opening routine, the sun beats down on the awkward apartment, enervating each one of the atoms in and surrounding the structure; this atmosphere consists of Nitrogen (78%), Oxygen (21%), and many other gases, including some Hydrogen. It might be assumed that the star is taking a vendetta out on the people below, but it does no such thing, for the sun remains a G-class star, burning at five to six thousand degrees Celsius, ninety million miles, or one Astronomical Unit (AU), away from earth, as it will for another 4.5 billion years. None of this matters to Trevor, who wonders about the late-night show and its illogical timeslot. More proof of chaos. He would ask Kat, but she has become catatonic with her mathematics, and to Trevor particularly high figures represent the number of times Kat's cheated on him, ratios equal the probability of her having some harmful disease …

Kat says: "Twenty percent."

In the East, Trevor and Kat were as indistinguishable as the molecules in a cloud. They could only be taken as a whole, could only be measured as a system.

Trevor tries to ignore Kat's numbers because the Cube, the precious Cube is much more important. It holds the key. Unfortunately, Trevor has never heard of Augustus Judd who, a mere six years after the Rubik's Cube was invented in 1974, founded Cubaholics Anonymous.

The apartment is a peninsula because it juts from the side of the main building, because it is for no discernible reason supported by raised piers like houses in Louisiana, and because there are floor-to-ceiling windows on all but the north side. Hence the structure, built obviously as an afterthought, is a protrusion of living space surrounded on five sides by pressurized and enervated gas. The windows to the east are blocked by bookcases containing Kerouac, Ginsberg, Burroughs, Keats, Byron, Hemingway, Fitzgerald, and other Romantics, Beats, and general adventurers. There are also textbooks, dictionaries, thesauruses, and a set of encyclopedias. Lying open on the floor in front of Trevor, who faces the eastern wall, is a volume of the encyclopedia. The article displayed is one about the birth and death of stars.

Kat once said: "We're gonna be stars, baby."

Trevor once said: "We'll shine as bright as the Dogstar, Sirius."

Kat once barked.

A wide view: to the south is the television, tilted because it is on an uneven elevated stand. The picture is snowy and shows a man with a large chin rocking his head back and forth as if it were on a spring. The set itself is placed dangerously close to the edge of the slanted dais. The room is chock full of items placed on the edges of tables, bookcases, ledges, etc., a veritable diorama of potential energy, giving one the idea that the precarious balance of the apartment, itself poorly stabilized on its piers, could be upset, could come crashing down if the proper force were exerted. Kat, on her mumbling ellipse, often comes close to disturbing the perilous construction of the room, but she hasn't quite upset the equilibrium. Yet.

The apartment forms a T, with the vertical portion

making the peninsula, the left portion of the horizontal being the kitchen, and the right the bedroom and bathroom. In the kitchen, the oven is on, pumping heat into the already stifling atmosphere. The windows in the peninsula not covered with bookcases are open, although they are held up by slight cords which could let loose at any minute; it is a blistering day outside. Also in the kitchen, all four burners of the stove are on, waiting to conduct heat into pots, pans, anything that may land upon them. Next to the stove is a microwave which is on the fritz, which continuously fires electromagnetic waves inside itself heating nothing at all. Adjacent to the microwave is the sink, where water flows and flows down the drain. There are light fixtures and lamps throughout the apartment, all turned on, but none furnished with light bulbs.

Kat once said: "There's no moon. It's so dark."

Trevor once said: "It's Kansas, what would you see?"

In the bedroom, pitch black because there are no windows, a hurricane lamp leaks oil onto the floor; upon closer inspection, the oil continues into the kitchen and the peninsular room, as if someone had been carrying the lamp around searching for something. Other than the lamp, there is an unmade bed, a fiercely rattling fan, and an alarm clock running on double A batteries incorrectly blinking 3:05 AM. In the bathroom, the shower and sink are both on, two different brands of electric shavers buzz, the lights (here there are light bulbs) are illuminated, and a blow dryer blows.

Throughout the apartment, the floor is covered with myriad books, papers, journals, notebooks, piles of drawing paper, cardboard, newspapers, magazines, etc. The density of the paper products at all points in the apartment is so thick it is impossible to see the floor. Footprints cover the manifold dross because of Kat, whose ellipse is *almost* perfect, but not quite; the detritus is also covered in ashes.

Amongst the debris on the floor is Trevor's now shredded journal which he kept during the trip West. Some pages near the kitchen read, "Our trip to the West begins with so much potential. Our car is filled with gasoline, our Zippos with butane, our coffee mugs with espresso. Our bobble-head doll's spring is compressed—all anyone has to do is push the button on the bottom and the toy's parts will shoot upwards, its silly brainpan bouncing around. The lure of the West, leaving everything behind for the Promised Land is intoxicating; we can hardly restrain the energy built up inside of our own bodies, let alone the various means of energy in our possession. Before we even leave our former driveway, Kat pushes the button on the bobble-head doll, and we laugh as the crazy thing careens around."

Trevor once said: "The road trip will be a grand experiment, although it will employ elementary cause and effect. In the East, we have stagnated. And whereas occasional dissipation is acceptable, final stasis is not. In order for life to continue, it must be put through the crucible."

Kat once said: "The cause for our stagnation in the East is comfort. Here we have our families, our friends, our familiar places. Our epic will purify us via unknown experiences."

To the west a window looks out to the Pacific Ocean. In the center of the room, facing the western window is a couch. A journal entry describes the scene: "Every night we sit here and look to the West, just like we used to back home. Now we see the Pacific Ocean curling, blue-green before us, always roaring inland, quietly sliding up the beach, touching the very sand of California, the Promised Land. We can only imagine that the water wishes it could freeze time and remain there forever, perched on the whiteness. And then, inexorably, it slips back, tumbling off of the beach and returning to the hulking ocean filled with memories of what was, filled with the soaring energy of the journey up that cliff which can only ever be made once before being sucked back into the aqua oblivion."

Kat says: "7.5×10^{18}."

Trevor worries he will never solve the Cube, will never regain the confidence of Newtonian physics, that his entire life will go by without him figuring out whatever he's supposed to figure out, that order will be lost forever; Kat continues on her kinetic ellipse and says, "Two thousand four hundred fourteen."

Trevor stops working for a second and says nothing.

§ §

Trevor once wrote:

"The East was a landscape disgustingly imbued with desperation, pathetically surviving on the chimerical hope of going West, but never making it. The Great Plains were singularly depressing because for miles in all directions the land was flat as if it had lain down to die quietly without dreams or memories, just one nigh-infinite blank space. Past the Plains, the Rocky Mountains, knowing they were next door to the Promised Land, soared to breathtaking heights, and much as any being that strives for greater things, the Rockies attained a majesty stemming from their desire to achieve California. And then there was the place itself: the Golden State. Where dreams came true. Where life was lived to the fullest. Where everyone was a rock star or a movie star or a TV star or some kind of star. No matter what your life was like back East, and everywhere was east of California, you could be transformed in the Promised Land. But beyond the Promised Land ... the world was so crestfallen after leaving California, it couldn't hold itself together. In a fit of geographical suicide, the tectonic plates cut off abruptly at the Golden State and dashed themselves into the sea – that blue-green abyss which forever and ever wishes it too could be a part of California, filching pieces of the Dream Land out of spite and envy. The ocean in its sadness and jealousy remains for eternity in a liquid, tear-like existence for being west of California. For west of California is Sheol."

§ §

For months after they arrived in California, Trevor and Kat stared out at that invidious body of water and felt like Balboa, who, in a manner of speaking, discovered the Pacific. After all, if you were looking at the ocean from where they were, that meant you were in the "Promised Land." But much as the landscape west of the Golden State lacked the energy to remain in solid form, the system created by Trevor and Kat was slowly being consumed by entropy (that can only increase), as they found that the West was merely another place on the map. The extreme differentiation they first perceived was replaced by an acknowledged and all-consuming sameness.

Their trip had been remarkable, but now Trevor and Kat tried not to think about those Romantic days. They tried not to think at all. With each passing minute, the energy that surrounded them, so easily harnessed before, was being abstracted beyond comprehension. And as the energy became more and more abstruse, Trevor lost all confidence in his

Grand Experiment, lost all confidence in definites like experimentation and mathematics, and saw the world as a chaos of probability. Cursing Einstein, Trevor became an obsessed shut-in, playing with his Simon or his Rubik's Cube, looking for answers where there probably were none. Kat, meanwhile, began bouncing from bed to bed, hoping to perpetuate the power discovered on the savage burn across the country. When she found only sex and the risk of disease, and once Trevor fell silent, she went numb, and, having once been a math prodigy (which she despised because her family forced her into ... Kat once said: "People should feel, not think"), she began reading about chaos theory, then delved into her old math textbooks.

Until they ended up where they are now.

Trevor says: "There are so many. But it must exist. It just must."

Kat once said: "You're looking in the wrong place. It's in the numbers. It's not happy, but it's in the numbers."

Trevor once said: "In the quantities, you mean. Integers, whole numbers, imaginary numbers. You'll be like me soon enough. Right now, you rest your hopes in the quantities."

Trevor originally played with a Simon, lights flashing like those in Las Vegas, simple sounds erupting from the machine. But the batteries, or so Trevor thought, had burned out. Actually, the speaker had merely gone bad. The Simon was still operational, still on.

§ §

The late-night talk show ends and a meteorologist comes on. He predicts a high-pressure front will move in. "Which means it's only gonna get hotter," the weatherman says in a strained, high-pitched voice, then flops his arms around like a bobble-head doll. Without air-conditioning or wind, although next to the ocean, and with the oven and the microwave, even to some degree with the stovetop burners and the blow dryer, the apartment is already diaphoretic, each atom in the vicinity moving faster and faster. Now adding in the high-pressure front, it would be as if the gases of the atmosphere were squeezing their way into the space occupied by Trevor and Kat, thanks to the ever-present force of gravity; and then the pressure of the gases, along with the pressure of the atmosphere and the proximity of the sun, combined with the small size of the apartment, would all work together to elevate the temperature in Trevor's and Kat's room to the point of fusion.

Trevor once said: "Always know the time, but never worry about it. That way everything will make sense, but you'll still have that feeling you're getting away with something."

Trevor says: "What time is it?! Why won't you tell me the time?! Why doesn't the sun die already?! It's always daytime, never night! Nothing makes sense."

Kat once said: "I never know the time and I never worry about it. I'm timeless, baby."

Kat says: "1.5 or greater in 4.5 billion."

§ §

According to T-symmetry, or time reversal symmetry, the universe is not symmetrical. It is, therefore, always creating more entropy, although the amount of energy remains the same. Hence, there is more interference than information, more chaos than dynamism. In the East, Trevor believed that his relationship with Kat would be similar, only that they would create more and more energy, while the entropy would remain constant. He has lived, however, to learn that the First and Second Laws of Thermodynamics always apply: 1) Energy can neither be created nor destroyed, and 2) Entropy tends to increase over time, and once created it cannot be destroyed. Because of this asymmetry leaning toward the negative, it is difficult for Trevor to remember the good times in his relationship with Kat. Anything positive is now shut out by the ubiquitous interference of the negative. Only bits of dialogue remain.

For a brief period, after the romance had been drained from California and the relationship, Trevor spent his days looking west, smoking cigarettes, and wishing the sun would explode into a supernova, blowing the earth to smithereens; occasionally, when she was not searching for a man with a new source of adventurous energy, Kat would join him—although she had no idea what Trevor was thinking about as he sat there silently, staring out at the sky and the ocean. Without causality or determinism, without control, life was unlife and all were undead.

Drawing further inward, Trevor imagined the time when the sun's explosion would collapse in on itself becoming a black hole which would crush all the remaining pieces of this drab planet into nothing. It was his last coherent dream before the mania of the Simon and later the Cube. Each day Trevor waited for the sun to begin its descent into the west so his visions of heavenly explosions could return, and at his behest, right before his very eyes, the sun would ignite into a blast so powerful it would rend this worthless planet into bits.

Kat says: "One trillion."

When he still had some coherent energy left, Trevor looked up "stars" in his set of encyclopedias. His heart raced as he read about stars that were torn to pieces by neighboring black holes, about giant planets engulfed in explosions so grandiose they made our entire nuclear arsenal look like so many bottle rockets, about mysterious pulsars firing encoded messages perhaps to other stars. But then he read about our sun. It was too small to go supernova. It was only a G-classed star. It would have to burn one thousand five hundred degrees Celsius hotter and be much more massive to erupt into the blast Trevor wanted. Instead, in about five billion years, the sun would expand out into a red giant. The red giant would extend past Mercury, Venus, and almost as an afterthought, it would reach past earth. The three planets would continue to revolve inside of the red giant sun. The new stellar configuration would remove the atmosphere; it would partially melt the mountains; it would burn off the trees, grass, hills, soil, and any other piece of nature; it would evaporate the water; it would leave the earth a desolate, golden brown as if it were a giant space cookie. Then the red giant would emit more gas and become a planetary nebula, later shrinking down to a fierce but impotent white dwarf, and finally it would recede into a black dwarf: a dead cinder. The earth would continue on, but it would be revolving around an exanimate ember of a star with just enough gravitational pull to keep the planets moving on their pointless elliptical paths.

Trevor once said: "I keep time for both of us."

After Trevor finished reading about the sun, he dropped the book in front of him, turned his chair to face the bookshelves, and began playing Simon, feeling that it must hold the answers since nothing else did, all the while cursing Einstein and his probability. What Trevor doesn't know is that Einstein did not like probability; it was Niels Bohr and

Heisenberg who accepted the notion.

Einstein once said: "I cannot believe that God would choose to play dice with the universe."

Bohr once said: "Einstein, don't tell God what to do."

Soon, Kat began her orbit around the room, walking in an ellipse that would extend seemingly over days and nights computing all the figures and formulae the world had to offer, extending out past Pi and remaining for ages with the imaginary numbers.

§ §

The colors spin around in their seemingly endless configurations. Each time Trevor believes he has solved the Cube, he finds he is incorrect; it then takes hours to approach the elusive conclusion. Perhaps he aligns the blue and the white sides, but the green and the yellow remain jumbled in a confused mass. Trevor understands that he could conquer the puzzle rapidly by tearing each colored square off the Cube, hence making the entire toy black; or he could carefully remove all of the colored squares and rearrange them so the red, orange, yellow, green, blue, and white are all perfectly aligned, but there is a principle at stake here, and since experimentation failed and certainty never existed, observation of this random event is all that remains. The Rubik's must be solved.

Consequently, provided Trevor never ends up at the same point twice, his solving the Cube could take 1400 million million years, given one second for each move and going through every possible configuration, since there are 43,252,003,274,489,856,000 possible configurations (only one of them being the "solved" Cube), which more simply put is 4.3 x 10^{19}. But what else is there to do?

Trevor once said: "Look at them all. There are maybe as many as grains of sand on the beach."

Kat says: "Astronomical."

Trevor once said: "We have a connection to them. The energy pulsing through us came from them. But we have to find a way to access that energy, to understand it in order to get anywhere."

Trevor says: "I don't understand! I just don't understand … anything!"

Kat says: "Astronomical."

Kat once said: "They're too far away. There aren't any connections to make. See those lights? The lights of the city, at the bottom of the mountain. Those are the only lights we ever need to worry about, baby."

Their energy had finally dissipated into the formulae and numbers which explained it. And the numbers which explained it were soaring higher and higher, perhaps increasing the pressure, perhaps aiding in the contraction of the cloud surrounding their apartment.

§ §

The book on the floor in front of Trevor, besides explaining the death of stars, also explains their birth:

"Stars are formed from clouds of Hydrogen left over from the Big Bang. During the formation of a star, before the star is born, it exists as an amorphous cloud of Hydrogen. Due to some outside force (a shockwave from a nearby supernova, contact with another cloud), and then due to gravity, the cloud shrinks in on itself. The pressure of all the gases heats the cloud. With luminosity, the stellar object becomes a protostar—the stage before the stellar object can begin fusing Hydrogen into Helium. As a protostar, the object burns with an infrared glow, increasing with maturation along the light spectrum until it reaches stability. The youngest visible stars are T Tauri, which often appear in binary pairs."

But when the star is in its amorphous cloud phase, it looks exactly like a planetary nebula, the stage in a small to mid-sized star's life right after the red giant phase. Hence it is almost impossible to differentiate between a star being born and a star dying, unless one waits to see what happens next.

The problem is that what happens next may not happen for years and years. But those who understand such circumstances can speculate on what might occur.

§ §

An errant book (*On the Road*) covered in lamp oil, sitting on the floor in front of the oven, will burst into flames. The fire will spread quickly, following the trail around the apartment, igniting all of the oil on the ground, in turn igniting the papers scattered everywhere and the coffee table, along with the entire stock of oil left in the lamp in the bedroom, the flames of which will set the walls and the bed ablaze. The shock of the ensuing conflagration will knock Kat off her nearly perfect kinetic, elliptical course, sending her into the windows on the west side (which will slam shut) and into an end table just past the windows. Upsetting the delicate balance of the apartment, Kat's collision will set off a chain reaction of falling ash trays, coffee cups, books, glasses, lamps, plates, silverware, pencils, pens, everything will crash to the floor. Between the fire and the cascade of precariously placed items, Trevor will leap out of his chair, and his Rubik's will fly, still unfinished, into the fire. When he sees the puzzle burning, Trevor will scream:

"No! There must be a center of energy where it all makes sense!"

He will make several attempts to wrest the puzzle from the flames.

Kat, frightened, will heave the burning coffee table through the western windows and leap out after it. She will proceed to lift the table (which will cool from red to white and finally stop burning, a charred remnant of the apartment) and carry it with her. Walking out past the rocky cliffs, over the sands of the beach, to the ocean, Kat will place the scorched table in the surf and begin limping around it.

After Trevor tries several times to reach into the flames to save the Rubik's Cube, the Simon will burst back to life emitting the angry, electronic pulse it emits when someone, unable to recall the proper sequence, has pressed the wrong color. Trevor, eyes staring incredulously at the game for a moment, will turn away from the Cube, which will melt into a black plastic puddle, the colored squares dissolving away.

Understanding that he must find a way out, Trevor will reach into the debris, come up with a plunger, and begin bashing his way to the East. He will scream, "There must be a center of energy somewhere! I know there is! I know it!" And as a chink in the bookcases is opened, as the windows beyond are broken, a faint, almost imperceptible red light will shine through. As Trevor continues bashing his way out of the burning apartment, as the entire place begins collapsing, the red light will become more intense, until Trevor is bathed in it. And when there is a hole large enough, still screaming about the center of energy, he will leap from his apartment in California into the much cooler air outside, into the focused red light.

The light will surge, engulfing the building, as the fire blazes and the awkward apartment finally falls. But even with the former apartment burning on the ground, the light from the east will continue to shine, although it is impossible to say which color. Depending, it may progress from red to orange to yellow to green to white and maybe, *maybe* even to blue, the color of the biggest and brightest stars, the stars that go supernova.

§ §

But that is only one possible future.

For now, Trevor remains in his chair facing the eastern bookcases, while Kat continues in her kinetic ellipse around the coffee table.

Trevor once said: "How will we know if we're wrong? What plans should we follow? What do the stars have in store for us? How do we access their power?"

Kat once said: "Just keep your head down. Don't worry about the stars. They'll take care of themselves."

Trevor says: "Oh … I think …"

Trevor once said: "It seems too easy. Too miniscule. Like … we'll wreck for not seeing the bigger picture."

Trevor says: "I think …"

Kat once said, laughing: "At least we'll leave beautiful corpses behind."

Trevor says: "… I've almost …"

Trevor once said: "Lost hope … in a vacuum … that will never return. It's just too big. Too much to think about."

Kat says: "186,000 feet per second, or c."

On the television to the south, the late-night talk show is long over; the programming has even moved past the weatherman. Now the set displays a show about inventors. Today's subject: Erno Rubik. Here Erno Rubik is pictured at the 1982 World's Fair, held in Knoxville, Tennessee. Behind him is a giant Rubik's Cube, perfectly aligned, except that the center is turning, as if by some giant, ethereal hand. Behind Rubik and his enormous Cube is the Sunsphere, built to signify the theme for that particular Fair: energy.

Trevor says: "I think I've almost got it …"

Back in the apartment, Trevor and Kat continue with their lives as the sun blares, as gravity pulls the invisible gases together, as the pressurized gas cloud rises in temperature, as the heat builds to an unbearable degree. What will happen next can only be guessed at. All anyone can do is wait.

THE CITY OF THE SUNSPHERE

At Heliopolis, we saw ruined buildings where the priests had lived. For it is said, anciently, this was the principle residence of the priests who studied philosophy and astronomy. But there are no longer such a body of persons or such pursuits. No one was pointed out to us on the spot as presiding over these studies, but only persons who repeated sacred rites, and those who explained to strangers the peculiarities of the obelisk*.

- Strabo
Geographica *(XVII.1:29)*

And now the new Sunsphere is the cynosure of Knoxville. Standing 6,520 feet tall, its base is a black, cylindrical tower capped by a circular crown that extends well past the parameters of the column accentuated by equally black spires which carry the eye to the orb. The orb is a perfect globe of gold hovering twenty feet above the crown. It rotates thirty

---

* Slightly altered.

times per second, 108,000 times per hour precisely as does the Crab Pulsar, located 6,520 light years away near the constellation Taurus in the center of the Crab Nebula. The Crab Nebula and the Crab Pulsar were created by the Supernova of 1054 (SN1054), although the exact date of the event is unknown. The Crab Pulsar is a neutron star six miles in diameter, far smaller yet much denser than the Earth's sun. Again, mimicking the Crab Pulsar, the Sunsphere's orb emits a concentrated beam of light that makes the sphere appear to pulse because of its rotations. If the orb could be decelerated, the light beam would match that of a lighthouse or emergency vehicle. The Sunsphere and the Crab Pulsar also emit radio pulses and X-rays, but only the X-rays are susceptible to Quasi-Periodic Oscillations (QPOs); hence the X-ray emissions vary, the light waves and the radio pulses remain constant. Once the Sunsphere was 266 feet tall, consisting of a green, girder-supported tower and a golden sphere made of connected hexagons. It did not pulse with light. It did not emit radio waves. It did not emit X-rays. It had a red light on a pole at the zenith to warn airplane pilots. On July 4, 2054, an explosion erupted around the Sunsphere, engulfing the structure in red, yellow, green, and blue flames. After the blast, a crimson and cobalt cloud was left behind. When the smoke dispersed, the new Sunsphere stood in place of the former. The orb began spinning. The city filled with light.

§ §

To the southeast of the Sunsphere, windows reflecting golden beams, is Knoxville City Hospital. In OR 1058, Yang Wie-Te, a second-generation Chinese-American, a physicist and astronomer, is in critical condition. He proved that the Crab Pulsar and the new Sunsphere are in synchronicity with each other. He is supposed to deduce the meaning of the cosmic alignment. He is supposed to translate the messages being transmitted through the radio waves, light emissions, and X-rays. He lies prone on an operating table. Whether he has solved the mystery of the Sunsphere and the Crab Pulsar is unknown. The operating room, contrary to the rest of the hospital, is painted white and the tables are stainless steel. The doctors, nurses, and assistants surrounding the astronomer wear suits of aquamarine, including facemasks, caps, and gloves. Their hands move rapidly. They speak in curt, terse commands or laconic repetitions. From the celeritous and ever-increasing activity, it can be deduced that the physicist is in a worsening state of dissolution. Should Mr. Yang die, he would be subject to the following penalizations: a $250,000 fine, the incarceration of his entire family in health resorts for the despondent and valetudinary located in Farragut (or Far West Knoxville), the marking of his entire family with the sign of the Theta (*theta* for *thanatos*, the death imprint). Yang Wie-Te's descendants will also be liable for any destruction caused by the physicist's death which could reach upwards of one hundred billion dollars to assorted insurance companies, banks, law firms, and other public and private interests. Ultimately, Mr. Yang's family may face the severest sentence: expulsion from the City of Knoxville. These sanctions, and perhaps more, would be effected if the astronomer should pass away because of City Code 529: Thou shalt not die, lest ye release a shock wave. And it is true, whenever a human passes away the corpse immediately releases a shock wave that ranges in power from a quarter ton nuclear weapon to a one megaton hydrogen bomb. On account of these puissant bursts, death is prohibited. With modern medicine, however, aging and dying are purely voluntary. Hence, no one has died in Knoxville in over twenty years. Yet a question arises: how could Yang Wie-Te allow himself to degenerate to his current status? No matter the reason, the penalties and fines to be exacted on Mr. Yang's family are theoretical, superfluous. At Knoxville's current population, and given the physicist's enthalpy and exergy readings, the shock wave from his body would be the genesis of a chain reaction of shock waves that would obliterate each building, that would eradicate the entire population of 100,000,000 Knoxvillians, if not the entire world.

§ §

Second only to the Sunsphere, Knoxville City Hospital is the tallest manmade structure in the city (since the aforementioned tower can no longer be considered manmade). From the roof of the sanatorium, the entire megalopolis is viewable, with the exception of parts of the Northern Wasteland blocked by the former World's Fair Tower. Here one can see that the majority of the population has clogged the streets, parks, bridges, sidewalks, riverbanks, and other open spaces of the city. Although the Knoxville Health Commission (KHC) inundates the airwaves, satellite signals, Internet, newspapers, magazines, etc. with calming broadcasts and Public Placation Announcements (PPAs), the news of Yang Wie-Te's condition has been disseminated by some means. Utterly docile, the citizens understand that if Mr. Yang expires, Knoxville, but more importantly the Sunsphere, will cease to exist. Yet the soothing tones, the conciliating reports, and the optimistic premonitions do nothing to alleviate the tension. In spite of the danger, such masses of people moved to Knoxville because of the new Sunsphere. Being a neutron star (although comparatively infinitesimal) like the Crab Pulsar, it supplies the megalopolis with an almighty source of energy. The citizens are also filled with this vigor. Consequently, no one in Knoxville needs to sleep any longer than three or four hours per night; only those who fight against their own inherent vivacity (which is also illegal) go without exercise; only those who eschew their intrinsic verve fail to accomplish their goals. Lassitude, as are aging and death, is a voluntary condition. Moreover, the Sunsphere provides the city with a constant heat source. The mean temperature in Knoxville is 85º F. Finally, much as neutron stars generate the most powerful magnetic fields in the universe, the Sunsphere's magnetism is due to its mystery and the mystery inherent in its connection to the Crab Pulsar. The answer to this enigma is what each citizen of Knoxville hopes to learn. Yang Wie-Te had been attempting to deduce the answer for over eight years when he was checked into Knoxville City Hospital by his assistant. He was found on the outskirts of the Northern Wasteland.

East of the Sunsphere, along Summit Hill, are Market Square and the Old City, until Summit Hill becomes Martin Luther King (MLK). Market Square and the Old City are an entertainment district composed of subterranean clubs: literally subterranean. Aboveground, this recreational zone is constructed almost uniformly of red brick. The streets are older, still molded from asphalt in most places down to limestone in others. Meticulous care has been taken in this borough to preserve an aged appearance of no particular year. Gas lights line Gay Street. South Central is made of brick. Advertisements for products no longer in use, whose use is no longer remembered are still prevalent. A structure rumored to be a saloon and a bordello in the middle to late 1800s continues to be both to this day. Past the Old City, the houses are concatenated, and yet most Eastern Knoxvillians still live underground. Whereas the citizens of Knoxville hope to solve the mystery of the Sunsphere, or to have the mystery solved for them, there are three cults whose beliefs find their origins in the exact date of the occurrence of SN1054, which explain their interest in the World's Fair Tower. The East is home to the Believers, also known as the Doomsdayers or the Apocryphites. They believe SN1054 was first observed by Sadiae Fujiwara, a Japanese poet, on May 29, 1054. Astronomers have proven that such a viewing would have been impossible because Zeta Tauri, the closest observable star before the supernova, was in direct proximity to the sun, therefore invisible. Furthermore, Sadiae Fujiwara was not yet born in 1054, since he made his astronomical hypothesis in 1235. Although the evidence is against their claim, the Apocryphites continue to believe that Fujiwara was teleported back in time to a position where he could witness SN1054. Along with this belief, the Apocryphites assert that whatever the pulsar message may be, it will encourage humans to die and be transported to Paradise, located in the Crab Nebula, to live with Sadiae Fujiwara and James Agee. The reason humans began erupting into shock waves and the reason the old Sunsphere became the new: so more earthlings would die simultaneously and be delivered to Arcadia. At this hour, while the city of Knoxville awaits the outcome of Yang Wie-Te's surgery, the Apocryphites have concluded that Mr. Yang induced from the X-rays what the Believers themselves already knew. Yang, who perambulated in the direction of the Old City about once or twice per month, was aiming to bring about the apocalypse when his turncoat assistant committed him. Asked how they are keen to such information, Believers will say that the X-ray QPOs "told me so." They will also say that the number *529* in City Code 529 is no coincidence. It signifies that the Apocryphite belief in May 29 is correct, that their convictions are also correct. Because of their obsession with death, Apocryphite temples are the aforementioned underground speakeasies. Here they lure Tellers, Ramponans, and their own kind to dine on deleterious cuisine, imbibe alcohol and other drugs, fornicate randomly, smoke cigarettes, brawl with their fellow citizens, etc. With their goals they are successful, although modern medicine, if consulted soon enough, can cure all of the effects of these activities. On occasion, since the diversions in these clubs are prohibited, the police launch cleansing campaigns, sending those who are found to health resorts; the subterranean caves, however, are labyrinthine and the Apocryphites have never been completely reeducated. Instead, they continue their rebellion, speaking of their apocalyptic revolution in hushed, deferential tones, pointing to the new Sunsphere which they feel was created when the ghost of James Agee rose from his grave to make possible the transfer of all humankind to Paradise. The QPOs told them so.

The Northern Wasteland was demolished by the only shock waves that have occurred. It is composed, solely, of rubble. There are no brick buildings. There are no skyscrapers. There are no cinderblock structures. There are no actual streets. There are no people. There is nothing but the reminder of what happens when a human being expires. There are sections where the detritus has been itself destroyed, leaving a view of the Appalachian Mountains far in the distance. The shock waves did not obliterate all of Knoxville because there were fewer people living in the city at the time. Before the explosions, the North was home to a fourth Sunsphere Cult: the Free Thinkers, also known as the Sunsphere Haters. Even with the radiating charm of the propaganda and the menace of death, the other Knoxvillian groups despised the Free Thinkers to an almost self-destructive degree. The reason the Free Thinkers were hated, the reason they were called the Sunsphere Haters: they claimed the message the Sunsphere was emitting meant nothing at all, that the alignment of the Crab Pulsar and the World's Fair Tower was a cosmic event of astounding, yet nonsensical proportions. The light waves, radio pulses, and X-rays were not a code to be decrypted, but even if they were they could be studied from the antipodes where there was no peril. The date of SN1054 is inconsequential, or was so to them. The Free Thinkers, therefore, worked to get Knoxvillians to apostatize, proclaiming there would be no revelation from the Sunsphere, that it was merely beautiful and dangerous. A scandal would have arisen if any of the Free Thinkers had lived: who caused the shock waves? Since the Sunsphere Haters were eradicated, they were blamed. The Tower, according to the other groups, had its vengeance. The one surviving invention the Free Thinkers imparted on Knoxvillian society is the Enthalpy/Exergy Meter (EEM). Exergy is the amount of energy that can be extracted from a system. Since this energy is ejected as a shock wave when a human perishes, exergy is the measure of a person's explosive potential. Enthalpy calculates internal energy, pressure, and volume (in the case of humans, weight). Keeping enthalpy low is the goal of all human beings who are not Apocryphites. A high enthalpy score means your body contains too much energy, too much pressure, or too much weight. Energy and pressure can add to exergy, increasing explosive potential. Weight cannot add to exergy, but an obese individual could still erupt into a shock wave equivalent to a quarter ton nuclear device. Furthermore, a corpulent human probably has a high energy reserve (since the Sunsphere energizes all), probably is under excessive physical stress, and both of these properties lead to a higher exergy rating. When enthalpy reaches a predetermined level (calculated by doctors for each individual) a person will either go into cardiac arrest or will immediately die; Yang Wie-Te was in cardiac arrest when he was discovered. The Free Thinkers, to simplify the EEM, wrote a song to explain its value:

> Enthalpy and exergy work together to instill harmony,
> Without them your deaths would destroy this here fine city.

The Sunsphere Haters hoped to preserve as many humans as possible until they could remove them from Knoxville. Members of the other cults now walk to the edge of Henley Street, which used to become Broadway in the North, whenever they question their own beliefs, whenever they lose hope in the Sunsphere. These questioners stand at the extremity of the city and ponder the expanse of the wastes beyond. In the distance, there are the mountains.

Fort Sanders, the University of Tennessee campus, and parts West are home to the Tellers of the Truth. Here there are mostly skyscrapers made of steel, aluminum, and prismatic windows which cast kaleidoscopic patterns. The streets are made of an advanced polymer that transmogrifies according to the climate to instill optimal traction. Along Kingston Pike, the largest thoroughfare in the megalopolis, are uplifting aphoristic billboards, appeasing colors, and tranquil professionally landscaped gardens. On each street corner is a speaker that broadcasts confidence-building adages and PPAs. Far West Knoxville is home to the mammoth KHC building, the third largest structure in the city. Contrary to the East, most Westerners live aboveground, as far aboveground as humanly possible, in order to be closer to the Crab Pulsar. The Tellers of the Truth, simply called the Tellers (or the Tattletales, depending on who one asks), believe the original Yang Wie-Te was correct (the Yang Wie-Te being attended to by rapidly moving, aquamarine-clad doctors is a far distant relative). He claimed that SN1054 took place on July 4, 1054. Since this date is widely accepted by the scientific community, the Tellers are completely confident in their assessment. They are also confident that, whatever the message may turn out to be, it will undoubtedly be found in the radio waves and it will undoubtedly encourage humans to live longer and longer. The radio waves hold the secret because they are the most easily deciphered. The secret is obviously to live longer because of the destruction corpses cause. Furthermore, the Tellers hold that their conclusions are correct because the old Sunsphere became the new on July 4: the date, they claim, of SN1054.

They also claim that the Sunsphere metamorphosis was caused by a blast from the Crab Pulsar itself. The fact that such a blast would have taken 6,520 years to reach earth from the Crab Nebula does not deter their doctrines. While the prognostication becomes grimmer for Yang Wie-Te, a one-time native of the West (who departed after the Northern Wasteland was formed), the Tellers believe he had yet to deduce the answer to the World's Fair Tower Enigma. He had been working too hard. He had worn himself down. What Mr. Yang needs to do, once he has convalesced, is to check into one of the health resorts, which are also the Teller temples. Citizens either choose to enter these sanitariums for their own fitness related reasons, or they are incarcerated into them when caught engaging in harmful activities often in insalubrious parts of town (the East). The propaganda from the city address system and the consumption of attitude adjustment pills, both Teller inventions, are not militarily enforced. A human who remains morose for an extended period of time, however, is considered to be engaging in antisocial (and therefore dangerous) behavior and may be subject to surveillance by the Knoxville Police Department (KPD). On this day, the propaganda and the pills appear to be inoperative, insufficient, since the general mood is one of consternation. Yet perhaps the propaganda is working, since the message transmitted for the past two days has been that the mystery of the Sunsphere was about to be solved.

Along Chapman Highway, south of the Sunsphere, live the Ramponans. The vast majority of their structures are made of cinderblock, but there is no architectural consistency. The roads are made of polymers, asphalt, cement, brick, and other substances. Some Southerners live underground, while an equal number live above to far aboveground. In sections their buildings are concatenated, in others they are sparse. The Ramponan ideology is that human beings can never really know anything at all. Facetiously, they uphold the SN1054 date "discovered" by Giovanni Lupoato, who backs the only Western recording of the occurrence which appears in the admittedly questionable *Rampona Chronicle*. The *Rampona Chronicle* itself includes an error, accidentally listing the supernova year as MLVIII (1058), instead of MLIV (1054). If this document can otherwise be trusted, and according to the Ramponans no one knows if it can, then the date of the supernova was June 24, 1054. Since irrefutable knowledge is solely mythical, however, the Ramponans proclaim they are ignorant of the actual date, but that the rest of humanity is also ignorant. Yang Wie-Te, vying to display his exergetic reserve, was equally benighted but had yet to construct a nihilistic detachment from his situation when his assistant committed him. Since nescience is the controlling factor for

Ramponans, they have no theories as to what the mystery behind the Sunsphere could be, any more than it is possible to infer the exact date of SN1054 (which might not have occurred in 1054). Moreover, while discussing humanity's witlessness, Ramponans will often declare that a doctrine of utter ignorance is itself a dogma, so humans cannot aver peremptorily their de facto state of naïveté. When dealing with Apocryphites or Tellers, Ramponans will frequently dismiss the X-rays (especially the QPOs) and the radio waves and point to the light, asserting that it is Morse Code. When asked what the Morse Code means they answer that no one will ever know. Often lacking congruity, the Ramponans feel their system is correct at this hour because Mr. Yang, who last resided in South Knoxville, is in OR 1058: a strictly ironic coincidence. The Ramponans remain in Knoxville to harass the other cults, to sow discord. Mockingly, they broadcast the radio waves emanating from the Crab Pulsar and the new Sunsphere. The sound, which is repeated ad infinitum, is a chopping sound, the sound of a helicopter, the sound of an overturned lawnmower. They intersperse these transmissions with belittling pleas of what it could all mean. In spite of their nihilistic detachment, the Ramponans also await the outcome of Yang Wie-Te's operation.

§ §

6,520 light years away, shrouded in a cloud of gases extant from SN1054, the Crab Pulsar sends forth its message encrypted in X-rays, radio waves, and light. For now, the Sunsphere relays its esoteric message, not yet deciphered, perhaps indecipherable. Yang Wie-Te was often known to gaze in the direction of the Crab Nebula. When asked what he was pondering, Yang would say that he was imagining himself near the Pulsar, he was imagining himself as an antenna, he was preparing to disseminate the directive that would one day surge forth from his brain. He claimed the Pulsar and the World's Fair Tower were made to speak through him. And they would. But now Mr. Yang is in the hospital, silent, perhaps awaiting his explosive transubstantiation. Yet in the Crab Nebula, the neutron star's nature does not change. It continues to pulse. It continues to transmit.

And now the new Sunsphere. Even below the structure, in what was once World's Fair Park, and what is now Sunsphere Place, people are compacted and waiting. They wait to learn of Mr. Yang's condition. They wait to learn about the mystery behind the new Sunsphere and the Crab Pulsar. They search for answers. They are told over a loudspeaker by a soothing, relaxing voice that the physicist, the astronomer is fine, that the mystery will soon be solved. Above them all the orb of the

Sunsphere pulses signifying doom, nothing, joy, nescience. Like the eye of a god it sees them all, the tower beneath standing as if a monolith to someone or something's past or possibly future demise.

Zeno's Shotgun Paradox

1) The Paradox of Place
"… if everything that exists has a place, place too will have a place, and so on ad infinitum."

- Aristotle
Physics *IV:1, 209a25*

Where you are: Nowhere. But everywhere is somewhere. Every place is someplace. Yet where you are: noplace. It simply does not compute.

So, you explain—

Before you, in a bluish light, a failing light, is a shotgun mounted on a wall. This could be anywhere, and if it could be anywhere, that is as good as nowhere. The shotgun is mounted on the wall in the room where you are standing. Scarcely more enlightening. The room where you are standing is in the house you purchased years ago. Yet where are those years? Where is your house? If someone asked, as they might, where you lived, you could not respond, "In the rooms of my house." Although, upon reflection, that answer is more truthful than any other. Perhaps. The neighborhood: Fort

Sanders. Random fact. And should you bring it up, you would most likely have to explain (oh, how you love to explain) the history of the name "Fort Sanders" (detail upon life-saving, life-affirming detail). But sooner or later, you find, "Fort Sanders" is no better than "wall," "room," "house." The city: Knoxville. The country: the United States of America. Alas, there are ten Knoxvilles in the U.S.A.: Alabama, Arkansas, Georgia, Illinois, Iowa, Maryland, Mississippi, Pennsylvania, Tennessee, Texas. You claim you are in Tennessee. That the continent is North America which, before the Panama Canal, was fully connected to South America. That these continents are in the Western Hemisphere (the western portion of a globe?). On planet Earth. That Earth is in the Solar System. That the Solar System is in the Milky Way galaxy. That the Milky Way galaxy is in the universe. Yet where is the universe? It must be somewhere. It must be someplace. Because if the universe is nowhere, then your precious details are meaningless. And what of the place where the universe is? And of that place's place? And of that place's place's place? And so on. Yet you persist: before you, you think, you believe, in a bluish light, a failing light, is a shotgun mounted on a wall. False. Before you, there is someone else. Someone who resembles you, yes. But not you. No. And before *that* person is a shotgun. If the dimming light can be trusted. Wherever it comes from. If, indeed, it comes from anywhere. If, indeed, it isn't an illusion (anywhere being as good as nowhere). An illusion as are "wall," "room," "house," "Knoxville," "Tennessee," "the United States of America," "North America," "the Western Hemisphere" (!), "Earth," "the Solar System," "the Milky Way galaxy," "the universe." And what potential can we find here?

Here? Where?

Where are you? Everywhere is nowhere. Everyplace is noplace. So, what can happen here? Everything. Nothing.

2) **Achilles and the Tortoise**

"In a race, the quickest runner can never overtake the slowest, since the pursuer must first reach the point whence the pursued started, so that the slower must always hold a lead."

- Aristotle
Physics *VI:9, 239b15*

Who you are: Sisyphus. And the one before you before the shotgun: Anton Ulysses. Yet character is defined through action. You, Sisyphus, are inactive. Your doing is the same as your not doing, and that, in turn, is your undoing. Who you are: no one.

You want to stop Anton Ulysses from reaching the shotgun. Previously, you *wanted* Anton Ulysses to get the shotgun. It was part of the plan. The foolproof plan. But now, you are not so sure. Now you want to stop Anton Ulysses.

The man before you. The boy before you. You can never view him as a man. To you, characters are not defined by action, but by thought. Boys are action. Men are thought. And you want to stop Anton Ulysses. You want to explain (oh, how you want to explain; oh, how you love to explain). You want him to understand. You want him to think. You want to overtake Anton Ulysses.

You never will. Anton Ulysses has the lead. And he will continue moving. He will continue acting. As is his wont. And in order to catch up, you must reach the last point where Anton Ulysses resided. And even if Anton Ulysses only moves a foot from that point, you will never overtake him. Because you will be in his last position; he will be a foot in the lead. And in order to catch up, you must travel that foot. Yet Anton Ulysses, always on the move, will no longer be there. He will still be in the lead. And on and on: Anton Ulysses progressing forward, you behind, no matter the speed. The father will follow in the footsteps of the son, ironically. You will be left behind. Anton Ulysses will reach the shotgun. Anton Ulysses will wrest it from the wall. He will spin around. He will point the gun at you. He will pull the trigger. And the blast will project outward. At you.

You? Who are you?

Sisyphus. No one.

3) **The Dichotomy Paradox**

"That which is in locomotion must arrive at the half-way stage before it arrives at the goal."

> *- Aristotle*
> Physics *VI:9, 239b10*

When it will happen: never. It must happen sometime. Anton Ulysses cannot be stopped. Your action is inaction. But sometime and notime are the same when you are only somewhere and therefore nowhere. No place. No chance. No time. When it will happen: never.

Anton Ulysses wants to reach the shotgun. Once he reaches it, his motives are unclear. And although you cannot stop him, still, he will never arrive. For in order to get to the shotgun, he must first reach the halfway point between his current position and the wall (wherever the wall is). And in order to reach that halfway point, he must reach the halfway point between his current position and *that* halfway point. And in order to reach that halfway point, he must reach the halfway point between his current position and *that* halfway point. And on and on. Anton Ulysses, always the actor, will struggle, forever if need be, will strive, heroically strive, will endeavor to complete his (Herculean) task. In vain. His journey, although it appears so brief, will expand. It will expand and expand. Until the shotgun appears miles away. Yet, mockingly, it is merely a few feet. So close by. So far away. A mission that seemed like it would take no time at all, takes an eternity. An eternity not to happen.

Happen? When will it happen?

Never.

4) The Paradox of the Arrow

"If everything when it occupies an equal space is at rest, and if that which is in locomotion is always occupying such a space at any moment, the flying arrow is therefore motionless."

- *Aristotle*
Physics *VI:9, 239b5*

(Anton Ulysses has the shotgun.)

What will happen: nothing.

(Anton Ulysses has the shotgun.)

Noplace. No one. Never. Nothing.

Even though Anton Ulysses has the shotgun. For, in order to fire the shotgun, he would have to cock at least one of the two hammers, either of which may break or prove defective, although the weapon is of high quality, because, sooner or later, everything fails. Then, once he has cocked one (or both) hammers, he must pull the trigger. With a smaller gun, Anton Ulysses would have to aim. But at this distance ... ah, but the difficulty of distance has already been discussed. So, perhaps

Anton Ulysses should aim. Provided that his aim is true, he would next have to pull one (or both) of the triggers which will unleash the spring(s) that has/have been pulled taught by cocking the hammer(s). Much like the hammers, the triggers and the springs could very well malfunction. Not to mention that to completely pull the trigger, Anton Ulysses would first have to pull it halfway halfway halfway, etc. The spring would have to move halfway halfway ... The hammers would have to move halfway ... And if, somehow, Anton Ulysses is able to get the hammers cocked, the triggers pulled, the springs unleashed, the hammers pounding forward, still nothing will happen. For the gun would have to be loaded, and the gun is never kept loaded. The gun is usually kept unloaded. It is possible that it has been loaded. The gun is loaded. You loaded it yourself. It was a part of the plan. Yet even with the gun loaded, the hammer still must interact with the shotgun shell. A shotgun shell consists of the primer (the explosive cap), the propellant (gunpowder), and the shot (made of lead). If the hammer strikes forward, it will hit the explosive cap (which must create a miniature explosion) which will ignite the propellant (if the gunpowder is properly packed and pure) into yet another miniature explosion which will perform the twofold function of (1) creating greater pressure behind the shot than the atmosphere applies in front of the shot (hence, sending the shot forward), and (2) fragmenting the aggregate of shot (unlike a bullet which is a single projectile). Yet the likelihood of any of this happening is low (see the previous sections). But even if it should happen, even if the gun mechanism and the shell mechanism all, against the odds, operate perfectly, still nothing will happen. For the shot must have been manufactured properly. Shot is made by pouring molten lead down a shot tower (such as the Sunsphere Shot Tower in Knoxville, Tennessee (wherever that may be) that is 234 feet tall and made of brick (to add more random details)). As the molten lead descends, air pressure makes it round (the taller the shot tower, the greater the air pressure, the better the product). The now round pieces of molten lead then cascade into a pool of water in order to cool. Once cooled, the balls, the shot is filtered through screens so the balls of the same size can be collected, so the irregular shot can be re-melted down, can be put back through the process. The chances of any of this happening successfully: zero. First, it involves a worker leaving his home and going to work (impossible); it involves the worker making his way to the container of molten lead (doubly impossible); it involves the worker ascending a tower (trebly impossible); it involves the worker pouring the lead down the tower (quadruply impossible); it involves the lead falling through the tower (quintiply impossible) and reaching the pool below (infinitely impossible) and then being accurately filtered through screens so manifold shot balls do not cause a shotgun jam (absolutely impossible). But even if this entire ordeal were possible (and it isn't … at all) still nothing would happen. For the principle behind the gun is that it will move lead through a target. Yet in order to move, the shot must not be at rest. Yet all objects that occupy a space are at rest whilst in that space. The lead which appears to be moving through the air, then, is actually stationary, and no more likely to injure you than the worker is likely to make his way to the shot tower early in the morning for another day of toil …

What? What can be done?

Nothing.

5) Paradox Solved

"The solution to all of the mentioned paradoxes, then, is that there isn't an instant in time underlying the body's motion (if there were, it couldn't be in motion), and as its position is constantly changing no matter how small the time interval, and as such, is at no time determined, it simply doesn't have a determined position."

- Peter Lynds
"Zeno's Paradoxes: A Timely Solution"

You are falling. You do not know how. You do not know why. Your arguments were perfect. Your logic, flawless. Noplace. No one. Never. Nothing. But just before you hit the ground, the ground which seems so far away, though it is not far away, as if you were descending from an airplane, you think:

only
the man
falling
from the
sky with-
out a
para-
chute tru-
ly knows
the dis-
proof of
Zeno's
Para-
dox

THE PHYSICS OF THE BOTTOMLESS PIT

> *"Once I am dead, there will be no lack of pious hands to throw me over the railing; my grave will be the fathomless air; my body will sink endlessly and decay and dissolve in the wind generated by the fall, which is infinite."*
>
> – *Jorge Luis Borges*
> *"The Library of Babel"*

A Deadpan Conversation

"That's a deep pit."

"Yes, it is."

"Bottomless."

"So they say."

"It's been proven."

"They used a rope."

"A rope?"

"A long, long rope."

"No bottom?"

"None at all."

"How'd it get that way?"

"No one knows."

"Just opened up."

"Just opened up?"

"Just opened up."

"…"

"That's a deep pit."

Proof of the Existence of Bottomless Pits

A man at a desk holding a piece of paper says:

"To prove that the Knoxville Void is actually a bottomless pit, a team of anthropologists and geologists determined where on earth the other side of the hole would be. With this location set, one part of the team lowered a rope ten times as long as the pit could be deep. Since the other team did not receive any of the rope, the Knoxville Void was declared a bottomless pit."

Footage of this action is displayed on a small screen to the left of the man.

Singularity

A man fell into a pit today. Dropped like a stone. It was the strangest thing …

He was walking slowly, randomly through World's Fair Park. Because of the sun-glare he could only be seen in silhouette. The shadow, like an optic disk in the atmosphere, played upon the world *almost imperceptibly. Then the earth opened beneath it. His hat floated around above the hole for a bit. But then it fell, too.*

Arguments for and against

Nicholas Copernicus, known for his Heliocentric Theory which proved that the earth was not the center of the universe, penned the original draft of what is now called the "Finite Planet, Finite Pit" Argument near the end of his life. Similar to the creation of the Heliocentric Theory, other scientists have since tweaked the treatise; the Copernican version, however, states the main idea: that earth is a finite planet, and therefore cannot contain an infinite structure. If by no other means, a pit that opened in the vicinity of the North Pole and continued directly through the crust, the mantel, and the core would still find its conclusion in the South Pole and the vacuum of space. Although technically it would be without an earthen bottom, the pit would still cease, since the entire expanse of space could not be considered part of the pit.

Unlike his Heliocentric Theory, Copernicus' bottomless pit article was not found until years after his death. In place of this pragmatic theory, manifold arguments arose and held precedence amongst various groups of thinkers: Plato's "No Shadow" Argument (stating that we could not see the shadow of a bottomless pit in the allegorical cave); Aristotle's "It's Not a Pit Without a Bottom" Argument; Saint Thomas Aquinas'

"Aristotelian God" Argument (wherein he agrees with Aristotle, but includes the Christian deity and Right Reason to the wording); Descartes' "Solipsistic Pit" Argument (remarking that since he was not falling through an abyss sans bottom, bottomless pits must not exist) which he later replaced with his "Good God, No Pit" Argument (proclaiming that a good God would not construct such a diabolical thing); Locke's and Hume's "What Pit? I Don't See Any Pit" Argument; Kant's "Categorical Imperative against Bottomless Pits" (elucidating the fact that since a pit could not expect all pits to be bottomless, no pits should be bottomless); and finally, Sartre's "Lack of Responsibility" Argument (quoting, "People fabricate bottomless pits in their minds so they need not take responsibility for their actions").

Until the opening of the Knoxville Void, the sole pro bottomless pit argument came from Saint Anselm, who deduced that, "Since we can conceive of no pit deeper than one without a bottom, then behold, bottomless pits must exist."

Observations on the Bottomless Pit

"Oh, they exist. You can bet on it. The government doesn't want you to think they do, but they *do*. They're everywhere. They can open up at any time in any place. You'll never know where. You could be walking down the street and

BOOM! a bottomless pit opens underneath you. And what are you going to do about it? A guy I knew put a map together of where all the pits will open because somehow he figured the conspiracy out, but the government came and took him away. He ... *knew too much*. They drove flying cars. They spoke in no human language. They wore all black. It was freaky, man. Freaky ..."

§ §

"Friend a mine fell inna one a them-thar bottomless pits. He'd been a drinkin' whisky and I done tole him to stay away from them-thar wells since they done got plenty bottomless pits around 'em. But 'ol Roscoe didn't listen, so's he up and fell in. Had to winch him out with ma truck."

§ §

"The Lord God in Heaven could, at any time, decide to cast all of us into the Bottomless Pit, and there is nothing we could do about it. Those who have Fallen, then, deserve their fate because it was designed for them by the Almighty; as for us, those who have not Fallen, we should get down on our knees and pray to thank the Lord that He has not decided to banish us into the Abyss."

§ §

"The Bottomless Pits, dude! They're the greatest band there ever was! I remember this one concert of theirs in Hotlanta, man, it was the best concert I ever been to. We were drinking beers and doin' shots and smokin' a little weed … not too much, man. Don't want to get roughed up by one a them bouncers. Those guys are huge … But the Bottomless Pits in Hotlanta, that was the most righteous show of all time. They played 'The Wind Will Blow' with that really cool guitar solo, and they did a cover of that Alice in Chains song, 'Down in a Hole,' and they did that creepy, 'Sink or Swim,' and 'Like a Stone,' and their encore was my favorite song of all time, man: 'Soar Above the Rest.' I mean what else could you ask for, dude? Guess they coulda played 'Ah-Ah-Ahhhh,' but … The Bottomless Pits and getting wasted. That's what it's all about."

§ §

"There are no bottomless pits. Not even the Knoxville Void. It's just a big hole. The whole infinite abyss thing is all a hoax."

§ §

"Bottomless pits? I'll tell you what a bottomless pit is: WorldRon. You have any stock in WorldRon? A stinking abyss if I ever saw one. People kept dumping money into it, but somehow it just all disappeared into the void. And all the money shoveled into the pit, well I'll be damned if it didn't turn into somebody's golden parachute. Like the mucky-mucks convinced the schmucks into jumping, but the mucky-mucks had jet packs and laughed as everyone else went screaming down, cheated."

§ §

"I have nothing but the deepest sympathy for those who have fallen into that terrible, terrible hole. Theirs is truly a tragic life. Falling for eternity, oh the horror. And if you will elect me as Mayor of Knoxville, I will do everything in my power to make the lives of the Fallers better, more livable. Hopefully, one day, we will be able to rescue the Fallers from their collective fates; hopefully we will be able to close up the abyss and make the future safe for our children. Indeed, I have a stake in this myself; you see, my brother fell into a bottomless pit ..."

Photonsphere

The mostly blue light of the television flickers on the man's face. He sits immobile, occasionally raising the remote to change the station. The current show tells him that the Sunsphere is a tower, 1000 feet tall, consisting of a glowing golden orb and a green shaft. Surrounded by static electric blue lightning because it channels energy, the Sunsphere shines day and night. Visitors are equipped with rubber suits to avoid electrocution. From the acme, visitors can view the Knoxville Void. Of particular interest is the nightly dance around the bottomless pit. Performed by fifty ballet experts dressed in bright white, the dance consists of a circle formed nine meters away from the pit. When the dexterous adepts move, it appears as if the hole is spinning and the dancers are remaining perfectly still.

What to Do in Case

It is, of course, best to avoid falling into a bottomless pit. But since most people stay away from them, it is unknown how anyone falls into one in the first place; and then, since those who do fall into them forget how ...

If you should find yourself descending through a bottomless pit, here is a helpful tip on what you should do:

Fall.

Fall with grace, with clumsiness, with aplomb, without any plums, with agility, awkwardness, dramatic gravity, comic ridiculousness, seriously, ironically, sanely, insanely, as if this had all happened before (likened to déjà vu), as if none of this has ever happened before, with religious zeal, with atheistic cynicism, with style and class, with churlish indifference, with purpose, haphazardly, as if you were born to fall, as if you had taken up falling as a pastime in old age, as if you were looking forward to falling, as if you always dreaded falling (but knew there was no escaping it), like your parents told you to, expressly against your parents' wishes, like a stone, like a brick, like a pillow, like a feather, like a feather pillow, like a penguin who thought he could fly, like an eagle who has forgotten how, with intelligence, with stupidity, like a dandy, like a tough guy, like Horatio Alger, like Socrates, not like Socrates, the way you were taught in school, as you learned away from or in spite of school, with a catfish, with any number of aquatic animals (perhaps they will keep you company), in the manner of King Arthur and his Knights of the Table Round, as a Shakespearean actor would, as a Samuel Beckett actor would, this way, that way, the other way, however you damn well please.

Just fall.

The direction in which you should fall: Downwards. Falling upwards is impossible, for falling upwards is flying.

Telephonic Repartee

"Hello."

"What?!"

"Hello!"

"Oh, hi!"

"How's the weather today in your part of the pit?!"

"Oh, fine!"

"Fine?! That's swell."

"Perhaps a bit windy."

"Well, you'll have that."

"Yes, you will. How about in yours?"

"Oh, fine, I guess. If you like that sort of weather."

"Yes, it is a subjective experience."

"That it is, that it is."

"So …"

"So, indeed."

"What are you doing today?"

"Well, I thought I'd plant some begonias and George and I were thinking of seeing a movie …"

"What movie?"

"Oh, maybe *Bottomless Pit*."

"I didn't know you were into action movies."

"Well, George is and I'll watch just about anything … It's supposed to have a love story in it, too."

"Oh … Maud?"

"Yes, Gladys."

"Never … never mind. It was nice talking to you."

"You too, Maud."

"All right. Goodbye."

"Maud? Maud?"

"…"

"Are you still there?"

"…"

Schwarzchild Radius

Occasionally, it appears as if there are an infinite number of channels which all show an infinite number of programs, but the variations between the programs are infinitesimal. The movies, the reality shows, the sitcoms, the soap operas, the talk shows, the science shows, the dramas, the comedies, even the commercials all blend together. And the man continues to sit in the blue light, occasionally raising the remote to add yet another modification of negligible proportions to the conglomerate program.

On the television, there are images of a botched construction project and this voice over:

"After the pit was found to be bottomless, the citizens of Knoxville decided that it would be best to seal the hole in order to keep people from becoming Fallers. An argument arose, however, in response to the fact that feathers in the bottomless pit supposedly allow Fallers to attain weightlessness and ultimately to fly out of the pit. It was then determined that a hole should remain, although a small one, an ocular escape hatch. During the construction of the cap, however, many construction workers and supplies were accidentally dropped into the pit. The project has been put on hold until a better plan can be worked out."

Terminal Velocity

An object falling through an atmosphere has a terminal

velocity: a point where the wind resistance upwards is equal to the gravitational pull downwards; once an object attains terminal velocity, it can travel no faster unless acted upon by another force. In a bottomless pit, however, terminal velocity does not exist because gravity exerts an exponentially increasing force upon a descending object. The Parallel Universe Theory of Multi-Dimensional Science explains this exponential gravitational increase. Obviously, it would be impossible for an infinite pit to exist within a finite space, much as Copernicus explained. Therefore, the overlap of dimensions containing parallel universes within the Knoxville Void makes continuous descent possible. For whenever an object begins to fall into a pit which contains a dimensional overlap, a dimension containing a universe exactly parallel to our own, that object will always, no matter the dimension, continue to fall through a pit that has dimensional overlaps containing parallel universes. If the falling object were to suddenly appear outside of an abyss, then that object would not have fallen through a bottomless pit, nor would it be entering *parallel* universes, it merely would have descended through a deep chasm with a universal warp inside.

As an object descends through a bottomless pit, each time it enters a new dimension, its speed is calculated as zero since the object is new to that particular time and space. Gravity, therefore, will begin to push on the object as if it had not been falling at all. This is similar to dropping a baseball off of the Empire State Building, and when the baseball has traveled the length of the building, someone catches it and immediately drops it off of another Empire State Building. The difference in the bottomless pit is that the "catching" is theoretical, is simply the entering of the object into another dimension. An object descending through the bottomless pit, then, is constantly achieving its maximum potential and kinetic energy states, since at any time it is falling as fast as it can, yet it is also in a state of rest compared with the force it will encounter less than a second into the future.

This state of maximum potential and kinetic energy coincides with the psychological assertion that Fallers experience a constant fluctuation of feelings, ranging from deep depression ("I am at my maximum potential") to high-flying giddiness ("My speed will forever increase from here").

Theorists do question whether or not objects descending through abysses, although they do not have states of terminal velocity, will catch fire and be torn asunder, like meteorites. Unlike meteorites, however, an object falling through a bottomless pit does not have to deal with friction. For once an object encroaches upon a critical state, it instantly appears in yet another dimension where its friction level is calculated as zero, where there is no danger, there is merely more falling.

New Fallers

No one remembers when he or she began falling (those who do are called *prevaricators* or *artistes*), or how or why he or she fell because of Faller Memory Degeneration (FMD).

If you are a Faller, when you first begin your descent into the bottomless pit, you are struck with the notion that you should not be plummeting through a hole, you should be ... But where should you be? You can't recall. A legion of facts and fantasies swim around in your disoriented brain, but you cannot sort them out; you cannot make sense of them. You feel as if your previous life vanished; or, more accurately, as if it were sucked out by a vortex, a black hole. Now you must deal with your predicament, but you have no idea how and no memories of helpful situations, similes, metaphors, anecdotes, pieces of traditional wisdom that can assist you.

As you fall, you look for the help of veteran Fallers. You descend faster than most veteran Fallers because you have not yet acquired any feathers. But you find the veterans to be of little help anyway because of acute cases of FMD. When you ask them about Falling, they look at you as if you were crazy, they tell extraordinary lies, they weave incomprehensible stories, they proffer useless bits of advice, they ignore you. Once you understand that veteran intelligence is worthless, you take to watching the veterans. In their movements, they are instructional. Here you discover the importance of feathers and debris, of the constant mood swings, of the various societies descending through the pit. You perhaps decide to become a Stone or a Toiler or a Flyer. Perhaps you don't decide yet. It's early. You're falling so fast. You're a New Faller. There is much to experience, although all experiences are difficult and subjective because of the soaring and crushing nature of your emotions. The combination of depression and giddiness is dizzying. The former emotion comes from the fear of death; the latter from cheating it.

When you first fell into the pit you did a great deal of screaming. You followed your screaming with periods of absolute silence. These reactions are normal, since you are in a constant state of vertigo where, although you are already falling, you forever believe that you are about to fall *again*. The veterans in the pit can be expected to either ignore your screaming, or to mockingly join in. Hopefully, early on, you will meet a person with a mild case of FMD. These rare Fallers remember everything but how they got into the pit and usually have control over their emotions; yet they are a somber group, spending much of their days talking to themselves or to their pets, wishing they could find a solution to this problem without an answer.

Accretion Disk

After watching television in a windowless room for a certain amount of time, the world falls away. The darkness of the atmosphere is ubiquitous and can only ever be penetrated by the blue. There is no universe outside of one's own. Experience and knowledge are the same, and both are attained through the box which, itself, vanishes; the images then play in the watcher's brain like dreams.

With a wry grin, the woman in the box says:

"Although the Rope Test proved that the Knoxville Void is bottomless, there is a group forming opposing the results. At this time their numbers are small. They are expected to march on World's Fair Park to refute the pit's bottomlessness, citing Copernicus' 'Finite Planet, Finite Pit' Argument."

The 8:15PM Showing of Bottomless Pit: The Movie

On the screen a cage is hanging over the bottomless pit, with a woman inside and a vile henchman outside whose hand is on a lever that apparently controls the cage's trapdoor.

"Oh, the Diabolical Villain's Henchman is going to throw me into the Bottomless Pit! Whatever shall I do," says Cleverly Bra-ed Heroine.

"Wooh-hoo!" says the Horny Teenager watching the movie.

"Smack," says the hand of the Horny Teenager's Logical Friend. "Can't you see it's all tape and padding, smoke and mirrors?"

"Damn," says the Horny Teenager.

"Bladow," says the .50 Desert Eagle, being wielded in one hand by Handsome Hero.

"Woh-ooooh. Ahhhhhh!" says the Vile Henchman, as he falls into the pit.

"Cool line," says Handsome Hero.

"My, Hero," says Cleverly Bra-ed Heroine.

"Boo! Boo!" says the Horny Teenager's Logical Friend.

"Not all people in bottomless pits are henchmen of diabolical villains," says the Credits of the movie.

"Aww," says Horny Teenager.

The Bottom of the Bottomless Pit

If you are a Stone, you fill your pockets with debris so you drop more rapidly. Owning no feathers, you sink even quicker than the New Fallers, descending through cascading communities, perhaps making friends, perhaps not, hoarding more and more items, who cares what they are? get all the debris you can, gain all the speed you can, you are a kind, reticent person and for the brief period of time you are in a community you help out in small ways, perhaps fixing something no one knew was broken until you quietly slip out without saying goodbye to anyone (at least not making a big production of it) and they say, well my goodness, I don't think this thing's worked in years, and the only long-term pals you have are other Stones who keep falling with you, but if they decide to become Toilers or even Flyers, then you leave them behind, making your own small transient community accelerating to light speed (which no one has ever achieved), always wishing for the conclusion, the place you will soundlessly and calmly descend to, the place that will mark the end of your falling, that expanse of beautiful turf, that soil, that ground, that base where there will be wondering why no more, that colorful, joyful, blithe zone where you will not have to undergo a dropping death leaving behind a descending decaying celeritous corpse, that land that lacks anxiety: the bottom. You wish for the bottom.

But there is no bottom. It's a bottomless pit.

Binary Pair

Steady breathing and drooping eyes show that he is only half-awake. Lethargy's hold tightens. An omnipresent buzzing sound, perhaps from the television, lulls him to sleep, absorbing his energy.

The blue says:

"The Finite Pit March, at first assumed to be a minor movement, is building in intensity. We take you now to our on-the-spot reporter."

A man with a spotty gray beard, backed by a star map says:

"The star HDE226868 taught us that the X-ray source Cygnus X-1 was probably a black hole. How did it teach us? Well,

for one, we found HDE226868 orbiting Cygnus X-1. Since HDE226868 is a supergiant star, whatever it was orbiting had to be more massive. Also, we found that Cygnus X-1 was actually pulling material off of its companion star. It moved, therefore, because something much more massive was tugging on it. That something is what we now call a 'black hole.' And nothing can escape a black hole, not even electromagnetic radiation."

"We seem to be having difficulty connecting to our on-the-spot reporter, instead that was our astronomy correspondent speaking about black holes. When we have a better link, we will bring you the news."

Speeches Next to the Bottomless Pit

"Why'd ... why'd you have to go and do it? Why'd ... why'd you leave me behind? You could've told me. You could've. Wasn't I always there for you? Wasn't I? Huh? Answer me! Please. Come on. Please. I don't understand. Why'd ... why'd ..."

§ §

"Hey, did someone order this pizza? Hello? Hello! I know someone ordered this pizza. There ain't any other bottomless pits in town. If you don't come up and get it right now, I'm outta here. I'm leaving. Just watch me ... Why do I always get stuck with the stupid orders to the bottomless pit?"

§ §

"What else is there? I've tried everything, haven't I? Now it's just so boring. A new life. A new chance. Something … It's gotta be better, right? Yeah. I figure. But I don't know. Who does? Anyone? We're all baffled. We really are."

§ §

"To be, or not to be …"

§ §

"If there is an 'Andrew Farkas' down there, and I believe there is, he still owes $250,000 on his student loans. If anyone can hear me, please let him know."

§ §

"Nietzsche says you're supposed to talk back or something. So … say something. You don't do anything. You're just a hole. And *abyss*, that's just a fancy word for *hole*. Don't go thinking you're all high and mighty, then … Well? Why don't you talk? Say *something*! I come here every day, sit on the edge, and talk. But what do you do? Nothing. You can change all that, you know? Tell me why I come here every day. Tell me! I want to know. You're not all that interesting, you know?

You're a hole! How intriguing can that be? Not very intriguing at all. And I don't care how deep you are … Caves. Now caves, they're fun. Hole, I hate to tell you this, but you're no fun at all."

§ §

"Wohh. Wo-oh-ohhh. Ahhhhhhhhhhh!"

§ §

"Deep enough for ya? Har har har har har!"

Personality Test Question
I believe bottomless pits exist.
1. Strongly agree
2. Agree
3. No opinion
4. Disagree
5. Strongly disagree

A Money-Making Opportunity

Jake Butcher, the bankrupt ex-convict who brought the World's Fair to Knoxville in 1982, is now attempting to become an energy mogul by harnessing the power inherent in the bottomless pit. He says that his plan will help the Knoxville community and the Fallers. His plan is to create Anthroelectric power, which will be similar to hydroelectric power; instead of rushing water turning turbines, however, falling human beings will be used to generate electricity.

"Anthroelectric power," says Butcher, "will be the answer to all of our energy problems. No longer will we have to worry about our depleting fossil fuel supplies, about how we will discover cold fusion, about destroying the atmosphere with our smokestacks and emissions."

By placing turbines at various points throughout the Knoxville Void, "We can harness this natural energy, thus giving meaning to the lives of the folks falling through the pit: they would be helping us by falling," says Butcher.

Since Knoxville itself does not currently have an energy problem, the Tennessee Valley Authority (TVA) would be able to store and sell the electricity to energy deprived areas, such as Los Angeles and New York City, which would in turn bring more money to the State of Tennessee. The TVA and the Sunsphere already power the entire Southeast United States. "Helping out the rest of the country is what we need to focus on now."

At this time the plan is still in the structuring phase. If it goes through, "We may be looking at a goldmine; we may be looking at the future of energy," says Butcher.

The Crushed State of Matter

Barely conscious, buried beneath many pillows, a voice rings out in the cobalt milieu:

"According to unidentified sources, both bottomless pit believers and non-believers are packing into World's Fair Park. The confrontation, non-violent at first, became a confused panic when a lightning bolt surged forth from the Sunsphere because of the collected heat energy and crashed amongst the masses. Several bystanders have been knocked into the Knoxville Void due to the hysteria. If order is not restored soon, it is certain that more will be trampled, crushed, and pushed into the abyss. Unfortunately, we have no video for you because we've lost contact with our on-the-spot reporter and we've been unable to hail any cameramen."

Feathers and Debris

"You know what I'm gonna do?"

"What?"

"I'm gonna get all the feathers I can find and fly the hell outta here."

"Really?"

"Will you take us with you?"

"Don't forget the little guys, right on?"

"I won't forget you guys. You're the best friends a guy could have."

"That's right, man. But how you gonna get the feathers? Some people take forever finding a couple."

"Don't worry about it, man. I got it all figured out."

"Come on, tell us."

"All right: birds. For some reason it seems birds fall like we do. So, I'm gonna catch the birds and take their feathers."

"Birds? Who's ever seen any birds at all, man? Ain't no birds."

"Ain't no birds."

"I told you, don't worry about it. I've seen birds."

"Oh, you're crazy, man."

"Fine, I'm crazy. What're you guys gonna do?"

"I'm goin' for the debris, man. Birds. Ain't no birds. I'm gonna gain all the weight I can and fill my pockets with all the junk I can find. I'm gonna head on out in search of the Zone man. The Bottom. That's what I'm gonna do."

"That's cool, dude."

"Ladies like Flyers more, man."

"Not true! I think the Stones are cool."

"Yeah, me too."

"Really doesn't matter to me. Figure we're all Toilers until one of us picks up speed or soars the hell outta here."

"You know what, babe?"

"What?"

"You're right. How you get so smart?"

"I don't know. Maybe I don't think about feathers and debris so much. Maybe more than everyone else."

"Lady, I don't care what you say, it's all about the birds."

"Man, you're high."

"That could be. But when I soar above all of you, you'll know where it's at."

"What, the weed?"

"Gotta live your dream, dude."

"Whatever. When you're flyin' around up top, I'll be chillin' on the bottom. No worries. No problems. No bottomless pits."

"Ain't no bottom, man. And there ain't no birds."

"Stop nay-sayin' us. We're just talkin' here."

"Yeah, I hear ya."

"What the hell was that?!"

"Looked like an Arthurian knight falling through the bottomless pit with a catfish."

"Not something you see every day, huh?"

"Maybe it keeps him company."

The Opening of the Bottomless Pit

Theoretical entities until recently, bottomless pits open in opposition to sources of infinite energy. The Knoxville Void, therefore, counters the Sunsphere: a monolith of power which surges with energy day and night, giving the city of Knoxville an eerie golden glow. Such a mass of positivity was bound to attract a puissant negativistic converse sooner or later. One of Jake Butcher's reasons for wanting to construct turbines to harness Anthroelectric power from the Hominefall in the abyss is to "turn the negative into a positive." This solution is problematic, however, because if both the Sunsphere and the Void were positive, they might either erupt into a magnetic explosion, opposing each other like the similar ends of magnets; or they might generate an anti-matter field that could transform into a black hole, tearing the entire earth to pieces.

Currently it is believed that the Sunsphere and the Void are in a state of balance, with the overabundance of energy from the gigantic gold and green tower no longer threatening local inhabitants (previously people had been electrocuted, some even killed by the stored static electricity). The bottomless pit's inexplicable appearance, although startling to the citizens of Knoxville, is figured to have taken place because of the surplus power seething out of the Sunsphere. When asked about the event, witnesses were unanimously unable to comment. All anyone could say was, "That's a deep pit."

Event Horizon

We still do not have direct contact with World's Fair Park in Knoxville. We have received conflicting reports from dubious anonymous sources. Speculation. The Finite Pit March demands to know where the information comes from. How lowering a rope into a pit proves it's bottomless. How we know people are falling through it. How we know anything about it ... at all. A hole in the ground. Theories. Theorists theorize. Actual evidence is necessary. Necessity is the defense of the believers. It must be bottomless. The Finite Pit March is swelling. It wants to know. Swelling. It wants to know. There is no direct information. The events are unknown.

Death in the Bottomless Pit

Fallers, although their bodies appear to follow different rules because of the manifold universes and dimensions they descend through, do die. The most frequent causes of death are asphyxiation, coronary, starvation, cancer, sexually transmitted disease, suicide. Asphyxiation occurs usually in New Fallers and aged veteran Fallers; for New and veteran Fallers alike, though, the reason for asphyxiation is the same: panic. The New Faller, believing he or she is going to hit the ground sooner or later, enters a hysterical state, either forgetting to breathe or hyperventilating, and then perishes; the veteran Faller forgets that he or she is falling, and undergoes the same process as the frightened New Faller. Coronary often accompanies asphyxiation for veteran Fallers. Cancer and sexually transmitted disease come about in the same ways they do on the surface. Starvation is rampant in the bottomless pit because there is little to eat. There are also murders and accidents. Strangely, there are no murders for food. Many of those who die of starvation have decided to expire thusly, assuming their lives are futile. The most common accident is careening into the side of the bottomless pit.

Because many people fall at similar rates of speed, and since corpses also continue to fall, Fallers are often surrounded by the carcasses of lost family members, friends, acquaintances, and even enemies. Some purposefully gather feathers or debris to escape these harsh mementos, while others remain among the dead. Those who linger with the dead either pretend they aren't in a high velocity morgue, or lounge betwixt the bodies as if they were normal houseguests. Those who pretend, on the other hand, either build structures around themselves to block out the carcasses, or remain in an eternal state of denial.

The most oft-cited example of impending death for land-dwellers is walking down a long, dark tunnel, and seeing a faint light at the end which grows in intensity. Not so for the Fallers. Imminent death in the bottomless pit is marked by an expanding, wide-open field where you can leisurely stroll in any direction; or, if you please, you may remain still. Movement in the abyss is compulsory. In the field, you can stop, you can survey the landscape, you can languish amongst the stationary scenery (which remains motionless except for the occasional calm breeze), without stirring, without advancing a single inch in any direction.

A Saccharine Love Affair

"So, did your son get the job?"

"What?!"

"Did your son get the job!"

"You don't have to yell."

"Oh, sorry."

"And no, I'm afraid he didn't."

"Why not?"

"Unfortunately, he 'Strongly Agreed' that bottomless pits exist."

"I suppose it's tough, since he is falling through one. How can you lie and say they're imaginary?"

"If he ever wants to get a job he'll have to!"

"I guess …"

"Listen, Mary, I didn't ask you here to talk about my son and bottomless pits."

"Oh."

"I have something to tell you."

"Oh-oh, Kyle."

"Yes, Mary. I love you."

"Oh, Kyle."

"I know the world is a difficult place and I know we're falling through a bottomless pit, but I love you. I love you, I love you, I love you. I don't care who knows or who hears, even though it's pretty tough to hear sometimes in the bottomless pit."

"Yes, it certainly can ..."

"Do you think you could ever love me, Mary? Even though we're falling through a bottomless pit?"

"Kyle ..."

"Yes, my love?"

"I ... I love you, too. I was afraid to say so before because it all seems so futile, what with the falling and the corpses and the heart attacks and the asphyxiation, but, Kyle, I love you."

"Oh, I'm so happy. I'd shout for joy, if the echoes didn't last so long."

"Oh-oh, Kyle, I'm so happy, too."

"We're in love."

"The greatest kind of love."

"A joyous kind of love."

"Even though we're falling through the bottomless pit."

Ergosphere

Awake. The buzzing noise, the pillows, the blue are still there. Continuing to maunder, the shows crystallize for now into the news. Every station carries the same program. The television personality, while shuffling papers, says:

"The Finite Pit March, again according to dubious anonymous

sources, has proclaimed that the bottomless pit is a hoax, that the scientific articles about the pit are shams, that the films about the abyss are purely fictional, that the television shows are likewise, that the bands supposedly slated to play at Songs Sung from the Edge of a Cliff *have not been contacted because there is no concert, and that the reason there is no actual news coverage of the conflict at World's Fair Park is because there is no one in the park. It is empty. When we have more information on this enticing story, we will bring it to you. We now return you to your regularly scheduled programming."*

The man in front of the television holds his remote aloft, but does not change the station.

Songs Sung from the Edge of a Cliff

To help fund bottomless pit research, a concert will be held at the Tennessee Amphitheater in World's Fair Park. The songs featured in the concert will be those from *Songs Sung from the Edge of a Cliff*. The title of this compilation album comes from the following: any song with, "Wohh-oh-oh" or "Oh-oh-oh" in it is sung by a person about to fall off of a cliff, and any song that contains a section of sustained screaming is by someone falling from a cliff. For instance, "Jamie's Cryin'" by Van Halen, since it contains the lyrics, "Wohh-oh-oh, Jamie's cryin'," is sung by someone about to fall off of a cliff, whereas "Immigrant Song" by Led Zeppelin is very obviously by someone who has already taken the plunge. The line-up for the evening includes many bands, most notably Knoxville's own The Bottomless Pits, who have both screaming and "Oh-oh's" in all of their songs.

The highlight of the show, however, will be Bruce Springsteen and the E Street Band performing their hit, "I'm on Fire," which contains Bruce about to fall off of a cliff right as he bursts into flames. One can only assume that after bursting into flames, he then falls from the cliff at the end of the song, though he is rather laidback about it.

His Pal, Sparky

"Sparky?"

"Woof."

"Sparky, you're my only pal, my best pal. Yes, you are; yes you are."

"Woof-woof."

"So I gotta tell ya, Sparky: I want to get to the bottom of things. Right to the bottom. Down here, we've learned that phrase means a lot more than we thought it did, didn't we Sparky?"

"Woof. Woof."

"I know, Sparky. But now that we're here, now that we've been falling for a while and we've learned all kinds of things about falling, I want to get to the bottom of things. You learn so much down here in the abyss ... Did I tell you where I heard that, Sparky?"

"Woof?"

"*Abyss*, did I tell you where I heard that? That one day when you were tired out and I took myself to the movies. Saw *Looking into the Abyss*. It wasn't so bad, Sparky. Naw, it wasn't. Not too bad at all. Kind of slow, not too much happening, just a bunch of people standing around a hole saying, 'That's a big hole,' or something like that, and then they all jump in at the end."

"Woof! Woof!"

"Don't worry, Sparky, they're just like us. They didn't get hurt or nothing, they just became Fallers. We're Fallers, Sparky."

"Woof."

"Thing is, Sparky, I don't know why they jumped into the pit ... oh, that brings me back to what I was saying originally: they called it the bottomless pit, and the pit, and the hole, but they also called it the *abyss*. I ain't never heard that one before, Sparky. Have you? Have ya, boy?"

"Woof-woof. Woof."

"Ya have? I knew you were a smart dog, but here you're a genius."

"Woof!"

"The smartest dog in the whole wide *abyss* ... But that's

what I want to do, Sparky. I want to get to the bottom of things. I don't know why them people in that movie, I don't know why they jumped in at the end. There's so much I don't know, Sparky. So much."

"Woof! Woof."

"Now you don't have to go agreeing with me so quick, Sparky."

"Woof! Woof! Woof!"

"Oh, I know. I was just kiddin' … But Sparky, there are so many things I don't know, some things I do know, but the one thing I really want to know is this here bottomless pit. I want to know what it is. I want to know why it is. I want to know why we're falling through it and why those people in the movie jumped in and I want to get to the bottom of things, Sparky."

"…"

"Yes, Sparky, go to sleep now. Let ol' Jay figure it all out. And then when you wake up, I'll've put it all together. I'll know why they jumped into the hole. I'll have all the answers. And then I'll tell you, Sparky, and you'll know, too."

"…"

"And then you'll be even smarter than a genius, Sparky … I won't be too stupid myself. No I won't, Sparky."

"…"

"And then [yawn], even though we're in the bottomless

pit, [yawn] in the *abyss*, we'll have gotten to the bottom of things, Sparky. Yes, yes we will."

Stationary Limit

Remote still held aloft, eyes transfixed on the television, the buzzing noise in the background louder, so he turns up the volume in time for the news to return. The man behind the desk says:

"Knowing that the television stations do not have contact with World's Fair Park, the Finite Pit March has sent us a videotape and a written message. The message says that the tape will prove that the pit is not bottomless. The recording shows—PAUSE—me broadcasting the news. I say that there is no bottomless pit, that it was all a publicity stunt to launch an already recorded season of television programming and films; that the newscasts concerning the bottomless pit are intended to raise ratings; the scientific articles were written by quacksalvers and researchers desperate for money; the guidebook explaining life inside the bottomless pit and the psychological profiles of those inside of the bottomless pit are also hoaxes. I say all of this.

"And then I play a clip from World's Fair Park. But the clip, strangely, does not coincide with the Finite Pit March's former claims: it shows a park slowly filling with people. In the background the Sunsphere stands channeling energy. All of the people hold hands and walk forward, but they appear not to notice each other. They act as if they were all alone. They form a circle *next to the Sunsphere. And in the circle the ground begins to dissolve, until an abyss opens. It grows larger and larger, as it swallows the participants. Many attempt to flee. But none escape.*

"Dear viewers, I do not remember making this broadcast. In fact, I remember so little. It's as if my mind was eroding away..."

Life in the Bottomless Pit

Falling through the bottomless pit, you become accustomed to the life you lead there, to the falling. It seems normal. You don't notice it most of the time. You even get used to the wind. It can be oddly harmonic, like a lullaby sung seriously by a comically tone-deaf vocalist. You speak loud when you have to speak. When you are with one of your friends, you sit very close and talk directly into his or her ear.

You spend a lot of time by yourself.

Perhaps you were filled with ideas of escape once. Perhaps you still are. The young always are filled with ideas of escape. It's normal. If you're not young, your dreams of escape are still normal because they hearken to your younger years. Everything is normal. Even dreams of life on the top, though you understand you don't remember what it was like there. Perhaps you have no interest in escape at all. Perhaps.

You are in a community of Fallers. You may be new to the community. You might be its oldest member. When New Fallers join, they believe they are on the fringe, and they speak in conspiratorial tones amongst themselves as if preparing for a prison break. The veteran Fallers, with their bad memories, assume the new members have always been there and have always acted strangely. In this way, everyone is accepted in the bottomless pit and everyone is an outcast; everyone is a part of the community and everyone is on the fringe.

You are a Flyer.

You are a Stone.

You are a Toiler.

You are and have been and will be all of these. Perhaps you have pockets full of feathers; you have pockets full of debris; your pockets are empty; some of your pockets are empty, some full of feathers, some of debris. And some pockets are only half-filled, but with both debris and feathers.

People are surrounded by garbage and corpses. From falling debris they build houses, where they read falling newspapers, eat falling meals, have falling relationships, work falling jobs, operate through falling days, and when night falls they try to pretend that they aren't surrounded by garbage and corpses. That they aren't falling.

Perhaps you explain to your friends what it is like for you. You tell them it's as if you're walking down a hallway. A long, thin hallway with doors on the far ends. You walk down the hallway. You open the door. You hope something magnificent is on the other side. Then it's another hallway, exactly like the one before. You continue. Walk. Open. Hope. Look. All the hallways are the same. But each time you open the door, you hope it will be different. It never is. So, you sit down in the middle of a hallway and refuse to continue. Yet the floor is a conveyor belt. The doors are automated. Against your will you go on. You don't see the hallways. You don't feel the doors. You don't look down the new corridors with hope.

Your friend, named Roscoe or Rhonda (you have trouble remembering who you're talking to), cheers you up by saying, "Deep enough for ya? Har har har." The giddiness returns. You will reach the top. You will get to the bottom. You will attain light speed. You will be the first person ever to attain light speed. At light speed you will expand to infinite mass. By expanding you will absorb everyone in the bottomless pit. By absorbing everyone in the bottomless pit, you will become everyone. The Everyman. Everywoman. Everybeing. Everyfaller. At light speed you will crush the fears and anxieties of the Fallers. You will be a star that was sucked into a black hole, but turned the black hole inside out and back into a star. You will be the cure for the incurable disease. You are the last best hope. At light speed.

Perhaps this feeling continues for hours. Days. Maybe only minutes. Before you descend back into your normal mood, if you have one. Perhaps Roscoe or Rhonda has to go. You are alone again. You cannot feel yourself fall. You want to feel it. You think of the top. You cannot remember it. You think of the bottom. You do not believe in it. Right now, you are a Toiler. At night. By yourself. You see no way out of your predicament, even though there seems to be no predicament at all. You have no idea what to do with yourself, so you accept being a Toiler. You accept your helplessness. You sit on the cascading floor of your house, in the middle of the floor at some time of the night, having been alone for who knows how long (were you always alone?), and you accept it all. No solutions. No dreams. Just you on the floor.

For now.

Tomorrow, there will be feathers. There will be debris. There will be the top. There will be the bottom. There will be the point, the incomprehensible point right before you attain light speed, where you will solve every Faller problem. And perhaps you will find all of these things tomorrow. Perhaps.

Ten Ways to Know You Are Falling through a Bottomless Pit
1. You fail to be impressed by the Grand Canyon.
2. People always say, "How are you … except for the whole 'falling through a bottomless pit' thing?"
3. Your favorite band has "Woh-oh's" and screaming in all of its songs.
4. Heavy objects levitate next to you.
5. You see the same people about all the time, until you load your pockets with bird shot.
6. Your number one greeting is: "What?!"
7. Wearing hats is just about impossible.

8. You feel as if you went skydiving sometime long ago, but something went terribly wrong.
9. You have been to many parallel universes and have visited several different dimensions, but you don't remember any of them.
10. It is very, very windy all the time.

Gravity Well

Completely aware, wide awake, the man in the blue atmosphere watches as his television reception freezes in place. And then the horizontal hold on the screen is lost. The picture flips ceaselessly. On the tube, the shocked and disheveled newsman, who was reaching out as if for assistance from his invisible audience, remains in the symbolic stance of one asking for alms forever. The picture flips ceaselessly. Or, perhaps more appropriately, it falls. With each passing moment, the man hopes it will stop. But it does not. He holds his remote aloft, impotently; squeezing the control with all his might, terrified to let it drop. For he does not know if it will descend to the floor, or if it will hover next to him defying all the gravitational laws, all of the universal laws he has ever known.

The Top of the Bottomless Pit

If you are a Flyer, you fill your pockets with feathers. Your descent slows. Old and New Fallers shoot past you. Your community, if you were in one, drops away. You are on your own. Solo. You wonder if it was a good idea. Filling your pockets with feathers. Your fall slows so much. You feel as if you are truly suspended in air. You have forgotten your descent before. But the wind. The sound of the wind was always present. For the first time it is gone. The silence roars.

You observe your surroundings. You look around as if someone has pressed PAUSE on your life. When you find you are still mobile, you are hit with a giddiness you've never experienced in your descending mood swings. You run back and forth. You collect more feathers. A gaping abyss is beneath you. You are stronger than the abyss. Gradually, you begin to ascend. First, it is like walking up stairs. Then like running up a hill. Like bounding off a trampoline. Like an express elevator. Like a rocket. The speed is intense. But you can handle it. *You* are intense. You are confident. *You* will make it to the top.

As you mount higher, the pit gets lighter. Full of light. Fallers gape at you. Ignore you. Some try to grab hold, pull you down with them. Some attempt to ride your coattails. Some attempt to stop you with their eyes. Their words. You outlast them all. You leave them all behind.

You soar above the rest. Above the Fallers. Until you're above the bottomless pit.

And when you're there, you see—

Do you wonder? Do you dream?

Do you realize that most Fallers dream of the top, but hope for the bottom?

Another Deadpan Conversation

"Why'd we jump?"

"I don't know."

"Pretty bad idea, huh?"

"Yeah. Yeah it was."

"What do we do now?"

"Fall."

"Fall?"

"Fall."

"Nothing else to do."

"True."

"This is a deep pit."

"Yeah."

"You can say that again."

"This is a deep pit."

No Tomorrow

"Who in this Bowling Alley bowld the Sun?"
- Edward Taylor

IDLE

FIRST GEAR

Man walks into a bar...

SECOND GEAR

... and maybe you know this already and maybe you don't, dude. It's just like learning to drive a manual. A stick shift, bro. When you're in first gear—the very first time, chief—it's a little shaky. Forget about the clutch, you stall the hell out. Grind some gears, end up ruining the transmission. But dude-man, it's like this: everything's all right. Solid. You got first gear down pat. Only sooner or later, man, I hate to tell ya ... you're gonna have to pop it into second gear. And what's that gonna be like, bro? You don't know yet. You just don't. There you are, dude, listening to the engine, watching the road, reminding yourself to hit the break and the clutch so you actually stop (which just never made any sense, *chief), and, like, how can anyone remember so many goddamned things? Tell me that, dude-man. So, when you hit that point when you have to shift out of first gear, the first time, life don't seem to be the happy-go-lucky place it used to be. It's all busted to pieces.*

THIRD GEAR

Since Comet Halley is so bright, one might assume that the substance burning therein is also radiant. This is not the case. The *albedo* of the nucleus of Comet Halley is 0.03, darker than coal; indeed, it is one of the darkest substances in the entire universe. *Albedo*, after all, is a measurement of the light reflected by a substance: 0.00 is absolute black, meaning all light is absorbed; while 1.00 is pure white, meaning all light is reflected.

FOURTH GEAR

In the bowling alley, Cal lifts his beer and laughs. The Custodian sitting across from him shrugs his shoulders, frowns, then smiles and drinks.

Cal leans back in his chair and watches as the solitary bowler rolls another gutter with the yellow-orange marbled ball. When Cal reclines, he feels something in his back pocket, something he must have forgotten about. The nuisance turns out to be a plain, blank white business envelope. Looking at the envelope, Cal turns and sees the bowling alley bartender, who is also watching the solitary bowler.

"Hey, look at this," says the bartender, and he removes a piece of paper that had been covering a freshly painted sign.

The sign says: FREE BEER TOMORROW.

IDLE
FIRST GEAR

His hair is dyed blonde, appears red in the sunlight of the doorway which gleams into the murky blackness, and ranges in curls around his head. He's gone when the door closes and the sun shines on him no more, reappearing throughout amidst the smoke and the dim light of the sun through blinds, neon, green shaded lamps, and silence. Artificial silence. No one moves. No one breathes. And even the thunk-thunk dissipates and dies before it reverberates.

At the door to the backroom, a netherworld beyond, the apparition whispers to one of the two sentries on either side holding pool cues like halberds, "The Samoan back there?" The sentry nods reverently. An envelope from his inside pocket is procured and the apparition is swallowed by the darkness.

A pool cue from within shatters against the wall, the apparition re-appears backwards, stumbling in reverse pursued by a beast of that netherworld who is an extreme of black and white, the white eyes glaring down on him. The beast swings another cue at the apparition, one of the sentries is now empty-handed, and roars with a guttural curse akin to no language and all languages. A supersonic explosion erupts as the silence is slain, and the apparition collapses to the floor. The Samoan shatters another stick and now both sentries are empty-handed, as the new cue stick whirls in windmill fashion, and the beast howls:

"Why would you try to hustle me?"

Before all goes blank the apparition sees a sign on the wall: FREE BEER TOMORROW.

SECOND GEAR

And once you're in the know, then that's the only place to go.

Because, well, dude-man, it's like this: It's all about the now, kid. The moment. Go as fast as you can. No one remembers yesterday and there ain't no tomorrow. *Right on? Right on. You know there's* no tomorrow. *You know it. I mean, when is* tomorrow? *When's it gonna* be tomorrow already? *When does* tomorrow *come? Was there ever a tomorrow? Do you have, like, fond memories of past tomorrows? Did you ever wake up in the morning, dude, stretch your arms and say, "Ahh, it's tomorrow?" No, man. You never did.*

THIRD GEAR

Sir Isaac Newton believed that the orbit of a comet was shaped like a hyperbola. If this were true, a comet would begin at a certain point in the galaxy (or the universe, depending on the type of comet), travel along an arch very likely with the sun as its vertex, and then it would cease to exist, it would extinguish once it had reached the other side. Hence each and every comet that came through our solar system was making its first and only pass; a brilliant, one-way journey.

FOURTH GEAR

As Cal and the Custodian walk into the seventy-lane bowling alley, their ears are hit by the profound explosion of someone rolling a strike. When they look at the solitary bowler, it appears that he is using two different bowling balls: one black, the other marbled yellow-orange.

"I bet you he gutters this one," says the Custodian.

"Why? He just rolled a strike," says Cal.

"A spare."

"A spare?"

"Yeah, look."

On the automatic scoring screen, Cal sees the Custodian's right: all of the Bowler's frames have consisted of initial gutter balls, then ten-pin spares.

"Anytime he rolls the yellow and orange ball he gets a gutter. Anytime he rolls the black ball, a strike," says the Custodian.

"Why doesn't he just use the black ball, then?"

The Custodian shrugs and the two men watch to see if the

theory is always true.

From the queue, the Bowler lifts the yellow-orange ball and with a few quick strokes, wipes the lane grease off with a towel. He hefts the ball in front of his face, looking down to position his feet between the first set of dots on the left side. Peering over the fiery orb to the boards, the Bowler finds his mark, bends forward, pauses: calm, immobile. With a fluid motion he advances into his approach. With sure steps and form, past the second starting-line (used by children and those with jerky sudden approaches), the Bowler gradually rears his arm back—a dance born of the dances of old, where steps and timing are necessary.

A breath before the foul line he lets loose, following through with his arm, hand stopping on the side of his head.

Sliding, not rolling, sliding, the ball slams into the right-hand gutter with an unceremonious thump.

Cal watches as the marbled yellow-orange ball warbles along the inescapable plastic pathway, an inexorable straight line that ends in an anonymous death. When it reaches the end of the ignominious trench, the fiery orb bounds into the netherworld behind the pins, rolling in plain view for a moment longer, as if it could return, as if it could travel the lane again and rectify the situation. And then it's gone.

THIRD GEAR

Edmund Halley countered Newton's argument, predicting that the comet of 1680 would return in 1758. When the comet did, indeed, return, astronomers realized that comets follow orbits, instead of being long-ranging meteors that burn out after one trip around the sun. Because of his discovery, astronomers named the comet for Halley, perhaps the most famous periodic comet in our solar system.

SECOND GEAR

Now you've got to listen to what I'm saying here, dude-man. I'm saying you have to, like, watch out for the Squares. Cause they're gonna try to slow ya down. Stop you dead in your tracks. Just the way it is. Doesn't even bother some folks, you know? They drive along, speedometer no higher than the limit. Even think they're getting away with something if they go five miles per hour over. It's sad. It really, really is, my man.

FIRST GEAR

There is dawn, wind, road, and then the car: a 1977 Mercury Comet, 302 v8, front end black, the rest marbled yellow-orange. A detonation, monstrous, of epic machinery, distortion due to the Doppler Effect. Hunkered down, bent forward, one hand on the gear shift, one on the wheel, the driver stares dead ahead.

On the horizon is the Sunsphere: gold, globular.

In the rearview mirror, barely perceptible, is a dark blue Crown Victoria.

Automobiles abound, the Comet zigging and zagging, slow lane, fast lane, turning lane, left lanes, the traffic parts and the Driver moves on, pushing harder, faster, never slowing down. The other cars are obstacles which influence his pattern, but not his direction. Until the Comet is in front of them all.

In the rearview, camouflaged amongst the other cars, is a dark blue Crown Victoria. No tricks of automotive genius can get rid of it. No skilled maneuvers can shake it.

An outburst of screeching rubber, and the Comet stops in a bar parking lot. At the big wooden door, he places an envelope from the passenger seat into his inside pocket. Sweat pours down his face. The Driver straightens his leather jacket, fading away in too much sunlight, solar conjunction too strong.

The dark blue Crown Vic drives by.

IDLE
FIRST GEAR

Golden light shining from afar, the always running headlights are halogen blue, playing off other cars, trucks, SUVs. From the radio, reception interlaced with static ... *which originate from the Oort Cloud, located 50,000AU from earth* and *the debris is left over from the origin of the universe* and *composed of lumps of rock covered with ice* and *of varying sizes, from a couple miles to several miles wide* and *they're rather like dirty snowballs,* where no topic can be comprehended until the program is taken as a whole.

Rounding a corner, the Sunsphere disappears, and the Comet is all by itself.

From the parking lot to Universal Trail, Ijams Nature Preserve is full of trees, bugs, cement, then mulch and dirt trails, plants, bushes, creeks, a river, green, blue, brown, green-blue-brown, the Comet Driver huffs and wheezes, slides, falls, leaves of every type, and then the sand of South Cove Trail, sweat, burning, the park is an undersea ruin with insects everywhere, until the sweat is wiped away. The Driver digs the heels of his hands into his knees, ambles up Tower Trail, leaves and mulch and dirt, leaves and mulch and dirt. Hacking, breathing, is there no acme to this hill?

At the crest sits a man wearing sunglasses, cell phone attached to his belt, drinking from a thermos. Not a drop of sweat on him. Not a drop. The Driver falls to the ground, seeing the sky through the canopy of forest. A copperhead crawls onto the Driver's chest, hissing, eyes locked on his.

SECOND GEAR

What I'm trying to tell you here, man, is: damn. With speed comes freedom. You've got to see life from 120 m-p-h. A new perspective, bro! A different angle. Like, spin it like it's never been spun before, dude.

FIRST GEAR

Visible from beneath dirt and mulch, some bugs, is an envelope.

The Comet Driver looks into the eyes of the snake. Snakes can hypnotize their prey into submission. The sunglasses man says nothing.

The snake hisses at the Driver, who lets his head fall back to look at the cold expanse of clouds.

SECOND GEAR

Might as well stay in first gear if you're not gonna feed the speed demon, man.

THIRD GEAR

A comet's tail always points away from the sun because it forms as the ice melts off the rock of the nucleus, and as the gas and dust contained in the nucleus are wrenched loose by solar wind radiation. From this process, a comet can form a thin tail (making it appear to be a streak across the sky), a thick tail several miles wide (which perhaps to us would look like a gigantic burning spaceship), or multiple tails …

"I have this nightmare," says Cal.

"Nightmare?" says the Custodian.

"Yeah. Goes like this: first everything will turn white and cold."

"You feel cold."

"Yeah, really cold. Like arctic. Antarctic. Slowly the white void starts to form into something: a cinderblock wall, a tile floor, a blockish easy chair. All of the colors in the dream remain washed out. They don't stay perfectly white, but they're always washed out. Until there's this blank room. No windows. No posters on the walls. No wallpaper. No carpet on the floor. It's just this blank room. Except there's a guy sitting in the chair facing a door."

"A door?"

"Yeah, a door."

"By himself?"

"Yeah."

"What's the guy do?"

"Nothing."

"Nothing ever?"

"Pretty much nothing. He just sits there and stares. Until gradually, he turns his head to me. He's got this vacant look on his face like he ran out of gas. No energy. He's just there. Sitting. He's got weight, since he's down in the chair. And he's taking up space. But that's it."

"Well that dream doesn't sound so bad."

"But to me it is. Whenever I'm having the dream … the nightmare, it's like I'm trapped. Usually I can tell when I'm dreaming and if I don't dig my dream, then I wake myself up. But I'm always locked into this illusion and I feel like one day I won't ever get out."

"How do you know it's a dream when you're in it?"

"Nothing like that could ever exist. The guy's so inhuman. His eyeballs are white with no irises. He barely ever moves."

"Now that's freaky."

"But that's not what weirds me out. It's just that there's this guy sitting there, never moving, just waiting at the door, and it doesn't seem to bother him. He's accepted this dissipation, he's accepted the cold …"

"The cold?"

"Yeah, it's freezing in there."

"Oh, white and cold."

"And stationary." Pause. "When he turns to look at me, finally, I feel like I'll be locked in his stare. And then I'll become immobile. I'll become him."

THIRD GEAR

On occasion, a comet's tail will appear to be pointing toward the sun: this is called an anti-tail or an anomalous tail. In reality, the tail only *seems* to be pointing at the sun. To form an anti-tail, the comet must produce large ("heavy") dust particles. If this happens, these particles are left along the comet's orbit, instead of being pushed away from the sun and the comet's orbit by light pressure. When the comet is rounding the sun, these leftover particles will shine and make the tail appear to point toward the sun.

SECOND GEAR

You know, man, we're gonna be the absolute best friends you ever had ...

THIRD GEAR

The time during which a comet is under observation is called its "apparition." For periodic comets, comets with more than one appearance, the term "apparition" is often used in conjunction with the year of its perihelion passage, such as "the 1986 apparition of Comet Halley." The term probably is derived from the ghostly appearance of bright naked-eye comets.

SECOND GEAR

... but only once you're going as fast as you can go.

FIRST GEAR

The Comet Driver spots the envelope, as his hand shoots up

and grabs the snake behind the head, hissing and tongue-batting, then soaring deeper into the woods. He hands an envelope to the sunglasses man, procured from his inside pocket, who reads the contents. When his cell phone starts ringing, the Driver unclips it, flips it open, then listens to the message, picking up the other envelope as he's on the phone.

When he's done, the sunglasses man says:

"You know why I come here? When I was younger, about high school age, I used to be really depressed. I started thinking that one day I was gonna die and I just couldn't imagine what it would be like to be dead. It was the scariest thing in the world to me. Yeah, I know, it sounds stupid. Every teenager goes through that. But I stopped caring about everything else. If something nice happened, it didn't matter because I was gonna die. I didn't bother to study anymore because a dead man can't use his knowledge to avoid death. I stopped talking to other people because they were all so stupid. They didn't realize they were going to die. They walked around as if this was gonna go on forever. Everything made me sick. I spent weeks, months in my room without doing anything at all, thinking I was about to die, focusing on the netherworld beyond. Finally, I decided that since life was so worthless, I would just throw it all away. I know that sounds like a paradox because I was so afraid of death. But my fear of death had been superceded by my fear of fearing death any longer. I was too scared to be depressed. So, I came up here to kill myself. Just as I was about to slit my wrists, I looked out at the river. The Tennessee River. I thought of the flowing blood and the flowing water. The river stopped me. It just flows. Flows right out to the sea. Into oblivion. One day it's a flowing river, the next it's a big mass of water. It doesn't care that there isn't any good reason for it to keep doing that. It just does."

The Driver looks out at the river for a few seconds with the sunglasses man. When he looks back, sunglasses man is gone—except for his cell phone and sunglasses. At the Comet, the Driver gets in and starts the engine. He doesn't see a dark blue Crown Vic pulling away.

In his rearview, he does see another trailing behind him.

IDLE
FIRST GEAR

A whoosh of yellow-orange, and the Comet is outside of a diner. Two doors slowly glide shut, and then the Driver in black leather and denim swings over the counter, hands the manager an envelope, answers the phone that starts ringing immediately. Behind the Driver, disdain, scowls, censures, reprimands, raised-voices, yells, screams of reproach.

The manager says: "What do I pay you for, you worthless son-of-a-bitch? Huh? What do I pay you for?" Waiters, waitresses, customers join—an amalgamation of insults. The Driver remains back-turned on the phone.

SECOND GEAR

Then let me tell ya, dude-man, between second and third gear, it really gets intense because you wonder what will happen in third and fourth. It ain't like first and second. In first, bro, you were a little shaky. Second, had to get used to wondering when to shift up, and when to shift it on back down. But in third gear, all you do is think about fourth. Cause you'll really be going fast then. Will you crack up? Will you die? Happens to all of us, kid. You just never know when. Like every second's gonna be your last, chief. Only way to do it. Freedom with speed. That's all, man.

THIRD GEAR

Comet Halley's aphelion, its most distant point from the sun, is 5.2 billion kilometers, and thus beyond the orbit of Neptune.

FOURTH GEAR

Cal sits on a bench in World's Fair Park, just outside the Knoxville Convention Center. He stares blankly forward. There is a Custodian lining the trashcans with bags. The Custodian looks over at Cal to see if he's awake. Then he points at the Sunsphere.

"Isn't that the ugliest thing you ever saw?" says the Custodian.

"What?" says Cal, shaking his head.

THIRD GEAR

Comet Halley's perihelion, its closest point to the sun, is 88 million kilometers, and thus less than one Astronomical Unit—closer to the sun than earth.

FOURTH GEAR

"The Sunsphere," says the Custodian. "That big, ugly golden ball in the air. Held up by them sickly green girders."

"Nah. I kinda like it. It's unique … or something," says Cal.

"If you say so."

"They said the same thing about the Eiffel Tower in 1889."

"You know what?"

"What?"

"They were right. It ain't such hot tuna."

THIRD GEAR

Comet Halley is a fine example of a short-period comet, taking about seventy-six years to complete one full orbit around the sun. It is not, however, representative of comets in general. Comet Halley is large, active, and has a well-defined orbit. Many other comets are small, inactive, and travel along eccentric orbits. Some even appear, much as Sir Isaac Newton theorized, to travel along hyperbolic paths, journeying through our solar system but one time. Astronomers believe that these comets are intergalactic travelers.

As Comet Halley is concerned, its eponymous connection did not witness its return. Mark Twain, who was born under the comet, did.

FIRST GEAR

Yells coming to a crescendo, the Driver still with his back turned, manager's spittle flying over the Driver's shoulder, waiters and waitresses behind the manager, cooks and grease monkeys behind the waiters and waitresses, customers behind the grease monkeys, all hollering and roaring some don't even know about what, and the Driver still talks on the phone, neck reddening, in a fluid movement phone slams down, fist slams into manager as feet spin body around. Silence. The delivered envelope floats in the air above the manager.

Silence.

A thunderclap as the envelope lands on the manager, the Driver flips out a new envelope from beneath the counter, vaults over and is out the door.

"Get out and don't ever come back," says the manager.

In reverse, the Comet sucked up by the road heads for the golden light.

A dark blue Crown Victoria pulls slowly behind.

IDLE

SECOND GEAR

… but you're not in control, bro. The car's in control. It shifts when it, like, wants to shift, you know? It thinks for you. It acts for you. Dude-man, all you're doing is turning the wheel. Sure, you had to get over the fear of all those crazy cars on the road—and what's up with them, man? And sure, I hear ya, loud and clear, you're getting used to how everything works. Only, chief, it's an automatic, it don't take that long. But you know what the worst part is? When you're cruising down the road in that automatic, my man, you think you're free. You ain't free. Not because it has to be that way, bro. But because you made it that way. You could've bought a stick shift. You could've been in control. You could've been king. Instead you got an automatic ticket to Squaresville.

Think of those Heaven's Gate cult-people, man. They turned all their control, all their freedom, over to some old bald guy— loony tunes like you wouldn't believe, bro. And look what happened to them. Don't be like them cats from Heaven's Gate. Don't give up your control and your freedom to, like, some guy who's gonna tell you lies about spaceships and comets. Do yourself a favor, dude.

Like, buy a manual. Then you're in control. You're free.

THIRD GEAR

Comet Hale-Bopp, a surprisingly bright comet, reached its perihelion on April 1, 1997.

FOURTH GEAR

"So this was after your dad was ..." says the Custodian, stopping with gravity.

"Yeah," says Cal.

"You didn't know the guy."

"Nope. Can't say that I ever met him in my life."

"And he'd call you up in the middle of the night and just start talking?"

"Uh-huh."

"He'd never wait to let you answer?"

"It was like he didn't want any answers. He wanted to talk."

"What did he talk about?"

"He'd talk about cars, mostly."

"Cars."

"But it was more than that. Or it seemed like more than that."

"Was he drunk?"

"He could've been. I really don't know. It was like I got a call from someone's brain and their thoughts were flooding through the phone, and instead of doing what most people would've done and hung up, I listened."

"Oh."

"After a while, it didn't seem like I was getting calls from someone else's brain. It was like I was listening to my own brain."

FIRST GEAR

He leans on the glass of a phone booth, other side of a hill, where the city can't be seen, phone balanced on his shoulder, obviously ignoring the call staring blankly forward saying nothing, listening not at all, there are hills, trees, shrubs, plants, grass, rocks, stones, pebbles, dirt, an infinite field of red dirt stirred into whirlwinds, miniature tornadoes threatening nothing at all, sun setting, red sky-red dirt fuse together in one vast, carmine presence, ubiquitous, a dimension before unknown, the whirlwinds amplify, the whole world sublimating into a scarlet universe enveloping the hills, trees, shrubs, foliage, rocks, stones, pebbles, the very dirt itself, until the landscape is choked with a sanguine haze shaped like Andromeda, earth becoming Mars, Mars becoming Jupiter, the phone booth is torn to pieces and dissolves into the red gas, and the whirlwind tornadoes are now a maelstrom that could either lead to a black oblivion or to a place that, by logic, should not exist, though belief in its reality is strong, until surrounded by the cerise vortex the phone erupts with that off-the-hook-for-too-long racket.

The Driver hangs up the phone, which immediately rings. He answers, listens, stoops and retrieves an envelope, leaves the phone booth, walks into the gas station. Re-emerging, the Driver, back in his Comet, speeds down the center of the street, road to himself in the darkness of early morning, unless the dark blue Crown Vics were far behind, lights off, invisible to the naked-eye, quietly delineating his progress.

THIRD GEAR

The head of a comet is called its *coma*. A coma is a fuzzy haze that surrounds the comet's true nucleus. All earthly spectators ever see of a comet are its coma and its tail.

The shape of the coma can vary from comet to comet; even one comet can have varying comae during its apparition. The shape depends on the comet's distance from the sun and the relative amount of dust and gas production. For faint comets or bright comets producing little dust, the coma is usually round. Comets, which produce significant quantities of dust, have fan-shaped or parabolic comae because the released dust particles are of varying sizes. The larger dust gets left along the comet's orbital path, while smaller particles get pushed away from the sun by light pressure. The smaller the dust, the more directly away from the sun the dust is pushed. With a distribution of both large and small dust particles, a fan is created. For comets within 1 AU, the coma of a dusty comet often becomes parabolic in shape. Clearly, for comets with fan-shaped or parabolic comae, there is no obvious boundary between the coma and the tail.

IDLE
FIRST GEAR

Behind the Comet are three dark blue Crown Victorias. A short, thin man is hidden underneath blankets in the back seat, unknown to the Driver. Sweat pours down the Driver's face as he approaches a citadel tower on a hill in plain view of the city. The Crown Vics make a three-point formation: a triangle. With a sudden movement, the Comet lances forward, cuts into a parking garage.

SECOND GEAR

Like maybe, man, you're like everyone else and you haven't driven a stick. You might wonder what it's like. What it all means.

THIRD GEAR

No matter what size the tail may be, there are two main types: gas tails and dust tails. Dust tails are prominent in comets that travel inside the earth's orbit, in regions where the warming solar radiation more strongly interacts with the ice in the comet's nucleus, causing much overall coma and tail activity.

FOURTH GEAR

Cal walks out of the Knoxville Convention Center. When he reaches his car, he looks at the sky. There is a shooting star.

"That's a Comet, right?" says an unfamiliar voice.

"Nope. It's a meteorite," says Cal.

"I mean the car. The car you're leaning against. That's a Comet. A '77."

"That's right," Cal says changing his view to his car.

"Great car. They should never have stopped making them."

Cal nods in agreement and turns to face a short, thin man wearing a blue suit and blue sunglasses.

"Where'd you get that envelope?"

"What envelope?"

"The one in your hand."

Cal still holds the envelope he had in the bowling alley.

"Oh. This envelope … I guess I don't remember."

"Would you tell me if you remembered?" trying to sound good-natured, spontaneous.

But Cal had turned his gaze back to the sky again, tired of the conversation.

"Well …" says the short, thin man, "it's a great car you

have there. Strange paint job, though."

"Yeah," says Cal, trailing off. Then he snaps his head up and asks: "Hey, who are you?" But when Cal looks back all he sees is a dark blue Crown Victoria driving away.

THIRD GEAR

Gas tails are more common and are more difficult to see. They emit light by fluorescence, in which gas atoms discharged from the comet's nucleus interact with solar wind radiation, re-transmitting energy received from solar radiation at different wavelengths. This fluoresced light in comets is very blue in color, which is difficult for the human eye to perceive. Comet Hyakutake was an exception, having a readily visible gas tail, and passing 0.01 AU from earth. Comet Hale-Bopp, on the other hand, was a very dusty comet.

SECOND GEAR

But, like, man, I can't tell you what it's like. You've got to find out for yourself, bro. Maybe that's what it's all about anyway.

FIRST GEAR

Up cement stairs, into hallways of magenta, green, light blue, past men and women dressed in white, or as clowns, or as daycare professionals, followed by a short, thin man in blue, the Driver moves on.

SECOND GEAR

That feeling, dude. Who cares about what it all means? Maybe you have to, like, make up your own meaning, you know bro? Who cares? As long as you keep moving.

FIRST GEAR

Doctors, nurses, equipment, beds, chairs, wheelchairs, crutches, machines (noisy and silent), a mass of anonymous patients, the Driver walks-runs, never knowing if there is pursuit, until he comes to a door. The short, thin man stops several paces behind.

The door is a vault door with a wheel, icy cold to the touch.

It opens with a clang, the short, thin man with eyes wide open. From inside a white light and a breeze of frigid air waft into the corridor. Puissant white light. The Comet Driver is enveloped. The whiteness set in contrast to the cheerfully colored walls. All colors are reflected, replaced by the ivory air. The Driver steps inside. The short, thin man attempts, but the vault closes.

A room, arctic, Antarctic, with cinderblock walls, tile floor, and nothing but a man in a chair facing a door. He stares blankly ahead, turns to see the Driver. His eyes are white, all white, and he shakily extends his arms.

He says: "My boy."

IDLE
FIRST GEAR

A man is asleep in the room where the phone rings at six in the morning. He mumbles in his sleep. *You're free*, he says. *You're in control*, he says. The sleeper rolls over, but doesn't answer the phone. The room is a bed, dresser, nightstand with alarm clock (green numerals, little after six), hardwood floor, no window, paneled walls, closet (door open), black corded telephone that stops ringing.

You're in control, he says. *Freedom with speed*, he says.

The phone starts ringing again. The sleeper rolls over and grabs it.

The sleeper doesn't move, then stands up, rubs his eyes, and he's completely awake. The phone call continues for a long time, then the man tosses the phone behind him, runs a hand through his reddish-blonde hair, enters closet, dresses, ambles out of the room. Everything's quiet for a few seconds until the phone starts making that off-the-hook-for-too-long racket.

Outside, the man looks around quizzically, shakes his head, gets into a 1977 Mercury Comet painted black and yellow-orange marbled. Keys are already in the ignition. The Comet backs out of the parking lot, pauses, then streaks down the road, black/yellow-orange, yellow-orange, yelloworange: a dot of color on the horizon. Then it's gone.

SECOND GEAR

... once you get to third, there ain't no stopping you anymore. All you want to do is get to fourth. That's where it is, dude. That's where it's at. Move fast enough, especially if you're in a sweet ride, my man, and the fears and anxieties of the lower gears melt away, right on? You're above it all. No one can stop you. It's so fast, there ain't any worries. Don't even feel like you're on the same plane with the other gears ...

THIRD GEAR

Since comets move about the solar system in elongated, often eccentric orbits, they spend the majority of their time far away from the sun. Deep in outer space, comets are frozen and invisible to our best telescopes. But just because we can't see them doesn't mean they're not out there.

FOURTH GEAR

The marbled yellow-orange ball emerges from the ball return and rolls into the queue right as the Custodian sets a beer down in front of Cal.

"Doesn't that bowling thing start today?" says Cal.

"You mean the big bowling conference?" says the Custodian.

"Yeah. Doesn't that start today?"

"No. Tomorrow. It starts tomorrow."

"Oh ... Hey, what time is it?"

"It's ..." the Custodian looks at his watch. "Well, what do you know? It is tomorrow."

IDLE
FIRST AND THIRD

Up close the 2003 apparition of Comet Mercury1977 appears to travel in a randomized pattern around the city of Knoxville. At this point, there is some question of direction from the telephone calls and the letters: the Driver always receives a telephone call, procures a letter, soars to his next target, delivers the letter. Perhaps he is a participant in a game, and perhaps he is playing his own game. For whereas his outbursts are bright, his core is dark. At point blank range the Driver appears to be so full of energy that it's draining off of him.

But from afar, at the center of his very eccentric orbit, is the Sunsphere. And even when he has gone beyond the sight of the Sunsphere, it remains his cynosure. Furthermore, much as there are comets that have had their orbits affected by the larger planets: Jupiter, Saturn, Neptune, Uranus, it may be that Comet Mercury1977 has also been affected by certain locations.

As for the tail/s of the Comet ...

They are always there. Visible. Invisible. Dark blue. Difficult to see with the naked eye. The tails are always there.

It's like they're these two guys, you know? and they're talking. Yak yak yak, yada yada yada. And the one guy says:

"No, no, no. It's unique. I love having that thing around. It reminds me that people don't always have to have everything looking the same way."

And then the other guy says:

"Well, sure, bro, I can see that. But couldn't they make something that looks unique but ain't ugly?"

And then the first guy, who is my main man by the way, answers back:

"Yeah, but that's just the way you see it. To you it's all ugly and nasty and shit. But to me, it's cool. Far out."

So, the second guy says:

"You hit the nail on the head, chief. To you it's cool; to me it ain't."

Then my man says:

"Yeah, but this is important, dude. You should dig that thing. Otherwise, you're just like the rest of 'em."

Second guy:

"Just like the rest of who, bro? We don't have to agree, you know?"

And then the first guy gets all mad, but then he calms down and says:

"Yeah, I guess you're right."

"Sure. Don't worry about it. You don't have to prove everything right now. Today. Let's get a beer in the Convention Center."

"Why not?"

The two men leave World's Fair Park and walk in the direction of the Convention Center that has a bar and, for a short time, a bowling alley. All in the shadow of a green tower with a golden globe atop made in honor of energy and stars. Many people, when the structure was first constructed, thought that it was a type of rocket ship. To date it has never taken off. But if it did, one would assume that much like bowling balls and comets and quite often people, it would return.

IDLE
FIRST GEAR

In West Knoxville, the windows of a house shake from the detonation of the Comet's engine as it glides backwards into the driveway. The Driver slowly gets out, walks to the front door, lets himself in. A man in his mid-fifties sits in a recliner at the end of a longish room, curtained windows, carpet, entertainment center, full of color, warmth, smiles at the archway leads to the hall leads to the door, where the Driver walks in and hands the man an envelope.

The man in his fifties takes the envelope, tears it open,

reads the contents. The Driver sits down tentatively on a couch.

When finished, the man says:

"It all seems like a dream now. Like it never really happened. Whenever I think about it, it's like I'm underwater. Like the whole thing is going on in slow motion. Like I'd made it all up. We hadn't spoken in some time. I was a drinker. An alcoholic. He didn't like to be around me when I drank so much. I turned tough. Violent. But that day, it wasn't my fault. Least, I don't think it was. Maybe it was. It's all so liquid now. There's one thing there's no question about: the Samoan was mad. Maybe he was a nice guy and I pissed him off. Maybe he was a jerk and he took it out on me.

"I don't know who, but someone took me to Emergency. They told me later I could've died. When they called my boy, he thought I was already dead. But I wasn't. Sure, I was in this dreamless darkness. Unconscious. Coma. Soon as I came out, though, I stopped drinking. Cause the only thing I could think about was seeing my boy. Only he didn't want to come to the hospital to identify my body. Like I said, he thought I was dead. After I got out, I figure he was mad. Mad at me. Mad at himself. Thought I hated him. Now I hear he's coming over tomorrow.

"Tomorrow. What a day that'll be."

The Driver points at a sign on the wall.

"I thought that was going to be the last thing I ever saw. That crazy sign: FREE BEER TOMORROW."

The man in his fifties seems to stare at the television, where the Driver looks and sees the sun glaring directly on the picture tube making another small, bright source of heat, energy.

In the Comet, the Driver pulls out of the driveway, notices a dark blue Crown Victoria parked there.

SECOND GEAR

Fourth is the tops, dude-man. Where it all takes place. So, go on. Get a move on, bro. On down the road, through the gears, engine roaring, tachometer flexing, speedometer don't even register that fast. You're flying. Living in the now. The moment ...

THIRD GEAR

Comet Halley's last apparition was 1986. It will reach its aphelion around the year 2024. It will return in 2061 and achieve its perihelion in that same year, or perhaps in 2062, depending on the accuracy of its orbit. But whatever its orbit, it will be back and will continue to reemerge to enrapture astronomers, comet watchers, and people who turn their eyes to the sky everywhere.

FOURTH GEAR

"You know, me and you should go bowling sometime,"

says the Custodian.

"Yeah, that'd be cool. I'm into bowling all right," says Cal.

"How about tomorrow?"

"Nah, tomorrow's no good. Gotta go see my dad. Haven't been in a while."

"Well, what about the next day?"

Pause.

"Sure. Day after tomorrow sounds great."

The Bowler is on his very last frame. His arm is tired, as he has informed his spectators. It is the first ball of the frame, so he hefts the yellow-orange marbled ball. Cal was just about to read the contents of the envelope, but instead he stops to watch.

"I hope he gets it this time," whispers Cal.

The Custodian says nothing.

With the yellow-orange marbled ball perched atop his fingertips, the Bowler gets into his stance, setting himself up as a paragon of tenpin excellence. Out along the lane, like an astronomer finding the pointer stars which signify Polaris, he locates his mark. And with a smooth, graceful motion, he begins his approach, legs gliding in sequence with his arms, which at the second set of dots drop down, the right arm then rearing back, and a breath before the foul line, the Bowler makes his release, following through with his hand to his face, his right leg crossing behind his left. Throwing what is called a "Brooklyn Curve," meaning although the Bowler is right handed, his hook starts from the left side, rounds to the right side, and returns to the left, the yellow-orange ball immediately heads for the right where it rolls perilously on the edge of the damnable gutter. Spinning along the precipice, the orb seems destined—preordained—to succumb to the fate of its predecessors. Rotating until the yelloworange form one color, the force of the hook exerts enough pressure, building enough friction on the lane, to finally grab hold of the greased wood.

There is a profound explosion.

For a moment Cal and the Custodian do not jump up in celebration, but stare at the pins and the yellow-orange ball. The pins lay on the lane; the orb rolls around in the netherworld. But it is not a netherworld, really. It is merely another point along a path. Then the pins are swept away, the ball disappears along its journey through the ball return, and the Custodian, who can wait no more, runs up to the Bowler and says: "Hey, nice one."

The Bowler says: "Thanks, dude-man."

Cal looks down at the piece of paper from the envelope. The paper, for there is only one sheet, is perhaps inconsequential, except for the beginning and the end.

It begins: "Man walks into a bar …"

And ends: "FREE BEER TOMORROW."

Everything Under the Sunsphere

The roads in Knoxville never end, the names just change.

It was the Summer of the Phlogistonites. That gang of arsonists who burned up the town. Scared the hell out of everyone. I was waiting at the intersection of Broadway/Henley and Western/Summit Hill looking at the Sunsphere when I first saw her. The Sunsphere is dilapidated. Some of the panels in the golf ball top have fallen out. They might still be on the ground, skidding through the park. She stood in the shade of a lone magnolia tree. Her hair was short and black. Black, the color of her clothes. Even in the intense heat (about 100°), she looked cool. Chilled. As if she had her own refrigeration unit controlling her bodily and atmospheric temperature. A quick glance at the lights, and then … But she was gone.

At the Sunsphere, which I visited every day, I walked down by the dried-out fountain trying to imagine what it's like when it's filled. I'd never seen it filled. The few stagnant puddles inside somehow made the weather seem even hotter.

I wipe away the perspiration with a pocket handkerchief I always carry. In summer, it's never cool enough for me. The sweat seethes forth in continuous rivulets, draining down my head, behind my ears, over my face. Soon the handkerchief is soaked through and I squeegee it off with my hands. A losing battle. I'll end up drenched no matter.

An out-of-body, out-of-time experience: me leaping into the fountain, plunging into the cool, clear water, saved from the sweat and the sun, never again assaulted by either of those caloric forces.

My apartment was no escape. It lacked air conditioning. And I lacked the funds to run air conditioning. So, the sun bakes my mind and its faculties boil over. This is a common story for me. There is a way to battle the torrid world, a way to understand it. But somehow, I'm on the outside. Even when the answer appears so simple, obvious: get a job that affords air conditioning; move to a place that has it.

I blame the heat. And my sweating.

Often I visit cooled places. But since I don't live in them … well, you can only stay somewhere that isn't yours for so long. My territory is the outdoors. I would sweat at my place just as much; might as well go where there's something to look at. The Sunsphere is across from my apartment. So I'm here every day. Even then.

A ritual I have: when I get to the Sunsphere, I press the

button that should summon the elevator.

But it doesn't work. Much as some of the golden panels are missing, much as the green paint on the shaft of the tower is flaking away. Nothing is in there anyhow. No one can get to the top. It's just a derelict reminder of the past. I pressed the button, no matter. I press the button and wait for the elevator to come down and get me, take me to the top where it will be air conditioned and I will understand everything.

While I wait, I look at the dried-up fountain. I might wait forever. Until the sun boils all the sense out of me. My end will be in a stagnant pool of myself.

In a shadow, in the distance, I saw that girl with the black hair, sitting on a bench.

"I just can't take this heat," I told her, sitting down.

"Why don't you go back to your place and sit in the air conditioning?" she said.

"I don't have air conditioning."

"This is the South. Everyone has air conditioning." From up close I could see she wore white lipstick.

"I don't," I said.

She turned and looked at me. Her eyes were probably sympathetic behind her sunglasses.

"What's your name?" I said.

"Sophia White. But my friends call me Stiria."

"Stiria? What's that mean?"

"'Icicle,' in Latin. What's your name?"

"Gene," I said, and shrugged my shoulders like I always do.

"*Eu*gene? 'Well born'?"

"Nope. Just *Gene*. 'Born'"

"Why don't you come back to my place, Gene? I have air conditioning."

"Cool," I said.

"Absolutely," said Stiria.

§ §

Then:

It was night. You could feel the fear in the air. The sheets stuck to me in the dense humidity. The temperature didn't drop at all from day to evening. All I could think about was people who didn't perspire. They wore sunglasses. Somehow they tapped into an ethereal icy source unknown to me. It imbued their entire existence. They would never sweat. No matter how hot it was. I see them and ask what I have to do. But they ignore me. I want to be like them. They're sleek. Suave. Knowing.

They're cool.

I turned on the radio. After the song, "The Heat is On," ends (a DJ's inspired joke), I heard:

It's been over 100° for an entire month now, in a crazy radio voice. I shut it off.

Unhelpful: the fact that during the heat wave, there was a group of arsonists at work. The first building to go was an apartment complex on Highland/Bridge. Only a couple blocks from my place. The heat from the sun and from the potential fire invaded my dreams. I would see the cool people with their sunglasses outside my window. And my building's on fire. Disinterested, they watch. Right in front of me is an escape route: a staircase. But I've forgotten how to walk downstairs.

§ §

Stiria and I would watch old reruns in her loft apartment in the Sterchi Building (a palace compared to my place) on State Street (one of the few roads whose name stays the same). We talked very little. She sat on the couch, still wearing her sunglasses, and I lay with my head in her lap. Neither of us ever got too warm. Maybe because she had the AC turned down to 65 for me. Maybe she was naturally hypothermic. For me, she was perfect.

In the chilled loft, I would slip in and out of consciousness. I am awake long enough to see an old episode of *The Dukes of Hazzard*. One where Beau and Luke are absent, replaced by men who resemble them, but who aren't.

"When I was a kid I felt cheated when Beau and Luke disappeared and these guys took over," I said.

Stiria didn't respond. She petted my head, as if trying to calm my overcooked mind. At the end of the episode, I realized that since I'd been in the South, I'd never met anyone named Beauregard. For some reason that bothered me.

§ §

Images of heat from that summer: a man jogging down Forest Park/Forest Hills. He was a marathon runner. Suddenly he falls over. He ran every day. He knew what he was doing. But his body temperature was 114° when they found him sprawled on the ground.

A car driving along Kingston/Cumberland/Main dings another. The two drivers get out. Without speaking, they fall into a fist fight. When another driver tries to stop the fist fight, he's beaten almost to death. The police use rubber bullets to stop the two men.

There is sun-poisoning. Heat sickness. Heat delirium. The inflamed, demented, diseased city runs wild. Careens down streets whose names change so often they have no names at all. Afterwards, people say, "It was so hot. So hot." And as atoms are enervated into chaos, people are morphed into demons. The city becomes hell. And the Phlogistonites thrived amongst them, burning buildings. So many buildings no one ever knew which was next. Everyone positive it would be theirs.

A man on the news says:

You know it's hot. You try not to think about it. You don't bring enough water. You're not wearing sunblock. The water boils out of you in streams you find annoying. You can feel how hot it is. But you don't think about your body temperature. You assume it will always stay the same. You don't think about how you're slowly dehydrating. You don't realize that you're slowly being cooked. And then it happens. Stick a fork in you. You're done.

§ §

A video shows Phlogistonite leader Paula Reddenbach (aka Paula the Pyro) speaking to her fire cult.

She screams and stalks about, her fiery red hair a mop soaked in sweat, her whole body soaked in sweat, she is covered with brown freckles, together a million, a billion fires blazing on her skin, firing her torrid purpose and she dances around the fire with the rest of her cult who are also covered in sweat, pressed together, generating more and more heat, the bodies sticking together, everyone chanting to the fire god or about fire or some scorched something that would inflame the world, a world half-naked, writhing, pulsating in the accumulation of bodies made into one with Paula as the shrieking, blazing head.

The tape ended with a close-up of the Pyro. Eyes aflame, a lurid grin on her face. As if she would devour the world with her inner inferno. I could feel the heat through the television.

I looked at Stiria, wondering why. But I didn't ask. Instead, I saw a reflection of a fire from the TV in her lenses. And I thought about the fact that in Stiria's loft it was always 65° just for me.

§ §

A guy pulled up and asked me how to get to Chapman Highway.

"You're on it," I said.

He frowned.

"No, no, no. This is Broadway. I want Chapman Highway."

"Right. But if you keep going, through Henley in downtown …"

"Turn right on Henley downtown. Got it."

"No. You're already on Chapman Highway. It's this road. It becomes …"

"What?!" Sweat poured down his face since the window's open in his car and the A/C's venting outside.

"This is Chapman Highway. It's also Henley. It's also Broadway."

"Son, what the hell are you talking about? Are you on drugs? Let me say it slowly. I want to get *to* Chapman Highway. We're currently *on* Broadway. How do I get to

Chapman Highway *from here?*"

"From here?" I asked.

"*From here,*" he said.

"You can't," I said. And walked off, wiping perspiration off my forehead, from behind my ears. But the handkerchief's soaked. So, I just ended up making myself sweatier.

§ §

Night. Sitting up in my room. Not even bothering to sleep. It's so hot. The radio's on. The fear in the city growing thicker. More buildings burned down: the apartments on Highland/Bridge, offices on Cumberland/Kingston/Main (also known as routes 11, 70, and 1), a short but wide school house where Magnolia branches into Asheville and Rutledge. The DJ says the Phlogistonites could be anywhere. No one was safe. The cops were clueless. At any time, we could burst into flames, erupt into madness. It had been over 100° for an eternity. People were already hot, irritated. Now, they were paranoid. If the Phlogistonites weren't captured soon, we would set ourselves ablaze.

§ §

A confusion of voices spilled into the hall. Everyone trying to talk at once. And it came from Stiria's apartment. I'd never met any of her friends. I'd never heard about any. Stiria didn't talk much. Whenever I came over, it's just me and her. Nobody called. Nobody stopped by.

When I knocked on the door, the room beyond went silent. I immediately thought of school. A group of kids would be talking. Then I'd show up. They'd go mute. Nothing to say. Weren't talking about anything anyway, why? And there's the door. Closed. As if it was open a moment ago. Only I hadn't seen it in time. So, it was slammed shut. Me on the outside.

A moment later, Stiria answered the door, adjusting her sunglasses, running her fingers through her black hair.

"Hello, Gene," she said.

Inside the place was a bit warmer than usual. Probably because of all the bodies. Or something like that. Stiria introduced me to everyone:

"This is Samuel Carrick, George McNutt, John Adair, James White (my cousin), and William Blount."

"Where's all the ladies?" I asked.

"Out scouting," one of them said. Then another shut him up with a punch in the arm.

The group seemed amiable enough. But everyone's awkward since they don't know me. Shuffling around, staring at the floor. They left soon after I was introduced.

"Tomorrow," they said to Stiria on their way out. She nods and lowers the thermostat to 65.

"Those your friends?" I said.

"Yeah. I work with them ... Oh, I think *The Dukes of Hazzard*'s on," she said.

For a second, it looked like it was. But it wasn't *The Dukes* at all. Instead it was some drawn-out infomercial pretending to be *The Dukes of Hazzard*. The actors only sort of resembled the people they're supposed to be playing. If you knew what to look for, though ... well, they're not convincing. The guys pretending to be Beau and Luke aren't even the second-rate copycats that filled in on the show for a while.

§ §

I was down near campus, where Volunteer becomes 16th, when Hodges Library burst into flames. It used to be a simple, squat, rectangular building. Then they pumped money into it. Made the library this sprawling, postmodern structure that reminded me of the old video game *Q-bert*. Now it's a charred husk. Q-bert could've still jumped around on it. Only he'd probably fall through.

The fire was fuel for more fear. Where were the Phlogistonites? Who knows where anyone is in a town like this? Who knows anything? The heat confuses everything; the fire devours all.

Amidst the crowd watching the conflagration, I thought I saw Stiria. Black hair, sunglasses. She's walking away. But as I tried to catch up with her, she walked faster and faster. Until I figured it must not be her. Just some girl who realized that this guy she didn't know was gaining on her. So, I stopped and thought of Stiria.

Stiria: her name, so mysterious, relaxes me. Cools me down wherever I am. She keeps me away from the heat, the burning, the scorching, the chaotic inferno, whether I'm with her or not.

§ §

More buildings got burned down: the hospital on Broadway/Henley/Chapman (also known as routes 33, 441, 44, and 71), the University Club on Concord/Neyland, a house on Forest Park/Forest Hills, and another place on James Agee, which used to be 15th, and following the order of the numbered streets, in a way still is. The buildings on the transiently named roads remind me that the University of Tennessee was originally called Blount College, that the Tennessee River somehow runs right through Fort Loudon Lake, so it's a river and a lake at the same time, and then it goes off and splits into two other rivers: the French Broad and the Holston, which makes me think about the flag of the State of Tennessee, which has three stars because at one time the State of Tennessee could have split into three separate states (West, Middle, East), and I'm sure somebody somewhere knows what the names of those states would have been if they ever came to exist. But that somebody isn't me. I don't want to know. I wish that the roads would have one name in one city. So, Kingston Pike shouldn't also be Cumberland Avenue and Main Street (along with the various route numbers it also goes by); it should be Kingston Pike and nothing else. When the road leaves Knoxville, it can have another name if the people in that town decide to name it something else. Same goes for the river. Cause, really, how does a river become a lake but stay a river, even coming out on the other side to be just a river again for a little while, before splitting into two other rivers?

It doesn't make any sense. Which makes me think of the fact that we didn't always have air conditioning. So, the problem for the namers was the same problem I have: too much heat. Too much chaos. Their sense was boiled out of them. Squeegeed away with their own hands. Consequently, they forgot what a street was called. Or if it had a name in the first place. And when all the naming was done, they didn't bother to change any of it. The various handles seemed sensible enough to them. Or something like that.

§ §

The police were everywhere outside of the Sterchi. They told me I shouldn't go inside. I asked why. They tell me I ought to go on home. Cops always want you to go home.

"Why?"

"It's just better you don't go inside, sir. That's all," said the police officer. Even in the uniform he didn't sweat. He wore mirrored sunglasses. I watched myself sweat in his eyes. I didn't bother with the handkerchief. I went straight to my squeegee hands.

Then I told the police officer that although he's a police officer, he couldn't tell me where I could and couldn't go unless there was a good reason. A detective overheard me talking, and came over. He looked at me like he was my dad. And he has really bad news. And he doesn't know how to give it. Another police officer whispered something to the detective.

"Yeah, that's him," said the detective.

To me: "Son, I think it'd be a good idea if you went home. Now, I can tell you you can't go in that building, son, because we got something going on in there we can't talk about right now, and I'm sure you understand what that means. We're not trying to be pricks or anything. It's just in your best interest to go on back to your place and cool off. Please, son?"

"Well, all right," I said. "But I can't cool off back at my place."

"Why's that?"

"I don't have air conditioning."

"This is the South," the cop said, distracted by something going on near the front of the Sterchi. "Everyone has air conditioning."

"Everyone," I said.

And I left.

§ §

The day after, I was back, ready to talk to Stiria about the whole thing. There weren't any police at the Sterchi that day. Outside, there weren't any people anywhere. Except for one guy who kept crossing and re-crossing State Street on three different corners. Inside, there were people everywhere, whispering. Like they had this big secret, and all of them knew about it. Everyone knew about it. But me. Only, it seemed the secret was about me. Whenever the people saw I was approaching, they stopped talking. And looked at me sympathetically, like someone had died.

When I got to Stiria's place, I had a lot on my mind. And it was all about roads changing names and rivers and lakes and cities driven insane by heat and paranoid by arsonists, and even about cops and what they think is in your best interest and how they always seem to want you to go home. The cops' paradise: everyone everywhere staying in their houses or apartments, never leaving. Which makes sense, now that I think about it. Less chance for crime, for chaos, for fires, if everyone stays at home.

The door was wide open. I walked through and it's like 120° inside. The heat knocked the wind out of me. Sliding against a wall, I found myself on the floor. Luckily, the loft had carpet. But that's all it has. Everything's gone. Even the TV.

Right away, I figured Stiria'd been robbed. That's why the police were outside the day before. Only I didn't know how you could get robbed of everything you own living on the eighth floor of a loft apartment building. Especially a nice one like that. Then I thought maybe she was kidnapped and her family's already shown up and taken her stuff. Really, that didn't make any sense either. When I could finally move, I ambled out into the hall and asked the first person what happened.

"Didn't you hear?" the guy said. My eyes were full of sweat, so I didn't see him too well.

"What?" I said.

"They caught the Phlogistonites. Turns out they weren't just arsonists, they were also masters of disguise and forgery. They stole a lot of identities. Used all kinds of names. Last bunch of names they stole were from the old Presbyterian graveyard."

But I didn't care about the names, so I interrupted him.

"Where's Stiria?"

Pause.

"Sophia White? The woman who used to live here?"

Finally, I got the sweat out of my eyes, although I still couldn't see too well. The guy looked like he felt sorry for me. It was just sweat in my eyes.

"She's gone, man. She's gone."

Later on, I found out that Paula and her band were arrested yesterday at the Sterchi. She was going to set it on fire, I guess. Or she ended up there after running from the cops. Which is why the cops were there when I arrived. The only thing I could think of: Stiria got so spooked by Paula she got the hell out of there but quick. Headed for someplace she could feel safe. Or something like that.

§ §

Walking through Market Square. To Stiria's. Before she disappeared. There's a party. One of those CityFest shindigs where cover bands play and business people drink alcohol out of plastic cups. And dance. And don't sweat even though it's like a thousand degrees out. But they're working on Market Square. They've got it all torn up. So there are fences everywhere. And I'm on the outside of the fence. And all the dancing, drinking business folks are inside. I can't find a way to get around the fence. There isn't a gate. I have no idea how they got in there. So, I stood on the outside and watched.

Wondering how to get inside.

At Stiria's I told her I either wanted to get in or I wanted to escape.

"Which one?"

"I wish I knew."

"I want to escape," she said. "I want to go far, far away where it isn't too hot or too cold."

"Why don't you?"

But she didn't answer. She put her arm around me. She was warm that day. Amazingly warm. She turned on the TV. It was my favorite show … When I think about her, that's the day I remember …

And now, I like to think Stiria slid across the hood of her car when she escaped the Sterchi. Just like Beau and Luke. The *real* Beau and Luke.

§ §

Of course, none of what follows actually happened:

The button glows red when I press it. I hear a whirring from inside. The fountain is still dried out, except for a few puddles. The park is littered with scratched, golden panels from the golf ball top. I am covered in sweat. Let it roll down my face. But the elevator is on its way.

There is a ding and the doors open. When I get inside, I see that it was all an optical illusion. Although the elevator appears to be opaque, it's actually glass. So, I can see the entire city as I ascend. I can see all the people and the buildings and the University of Tennessee (Blount College) and all of the variously named and route numbered streets.

On the way up: I like to think that I was made in God's own image. That God is just as awkward, and ridiculous, and sweaty as me, that He has so many names because He's too timid to tell anyone they're wrong, that His real name is …

When I get to the top, I find myself in an all white room made of cinderblocks. I don't understand how the inside of the Sunsphere can be made of cinderblocks, but it is. There is no air conditioning. In the room, there is a man sitting in a chair. He looks like a burned out, confused, sweaty version of Colonel Sanders. The author of my story. For fun, I'll call him Beauregard.

He offers me some fried chicken.

I ask how come the inside of the Sunsphere isn't gold. It becomes gold. Even in the heat, I'm cheered up a little by this.

Then we look at the world through the golden glass. Me and Beauregard. Neither one of us knows what to do in this world. Neither one of us knows how to make sense of it. Our sense has been boiled away in the heat. Squeegeed away by our own hands. But for a brief moment, me and Beauregard make a connection. Because just as I am about to ask, Beauregard makes it come true. And suddenly, from the

Sunsphere, that broken-down remnant of the past, we're able to look past the city of Knoxville, we're able to look past all of it, and we're able to see the place where the roads run logically and the streets' names never change.

WHITE DWARF BLUES

Believe you me, I know what kind of story this is: this is one of those peppy, cheery, happy, pick-me-up, feel-good stories where someone keeps doing something over and over until it kills him. A drug noir story. And aren't you lucky, you're reading it! And aren't I lucky, I'm the main character who's offing ... You don't know what a drug noir story is? Well! Let me tell you—

Think of Hubert Selby, Jr's *Requiem for a Dream*. Think of Irvine Welsh's *Trainspotting*. Think of Bret Easton Ellis' *Less Than Zero*. Think of the films *Leaving Las Vegas* or *Sid and Nancy*. Then you'll have a good idea[1].

For the sake of economy, I will be your narrator and main character. Yes, I exist in the present and speak of the past and the present. And if you think you can't trust me cuz junkies always lie, cuz druggies think they're in control when they're

---

[1] I'm so excited to be in my own drug noir! I love it! And when I say I love it, of course I mean I can't stand it, hate it, despise it, cuz that's the kind of attitude ya need in a drug noir – surly.

not, well, let me let you in on a little secret: I'm not really addicted cuz I can quit whenever I want. Anyway, how can this be wrong when it feels so right? See, I can play both sides—the reliable narrator and the deluded junky. So, don't worry. You can trust me from the beginning (which isn't here yet) to the inevitable downer ending (oh, I can't wait), in this my drug noir.

§ §

So, where are we? And what drugs are we talking about here? Heroin in NYC? Alcohol in Vegas? Cocaine in LA? Acid in San Francisco (a hippie noir!)? Oh, no. Not at all. I'm different. Where am I? Knoxville, Tennessee. And what's my suicide of choice …?

Oh, I know it's not the most romantic death. It's not a hip, happening, with-it demise. You don't hear the kids talking in hush-hush tones about getting my drug, admiration in their voices, envy on their lips, dreams in their twisted little heads, tell-all confessional stories whispered in a sexy susurrus about sordid deals and strung-out nights on _____ that they couldn't even … get to the point? Okay!

To kill myself, in this cheery tale, I'm eating all my meals at Captain D's.

That's right.

The fried fish place!

It's not a sexy fix, but it's mine.

§ §

The beginning: sitting in Captain D's waiting for Freddie Bessel to saunter in. We don't know each other yet, but he's gonna come in wearing all black except for a yellow-orange shirt. You see, up till now, my story hasn't taken off (although I'm already a white dwarf!) cuz I haven't had anyone to start a plot with. In a drug noir, the protagonist either has a buddy who's on a similar doomed path, or a significant other who wants to change the mainman's ways. Drug noirs involve binary pairs, not solo stars. And what better place to start than at …

You don't think Captain D's is sordid? Oh! That's because you've never been to *my* Captain D's. Here's the full experience:

It looks like a punk rock bar. Walking in through the scarred, black, wooden doors, the normally polished floors are filthy; the lights, dim; the shadows, deep. The ship décor isn't "yacht club," it's "the docks"—where shady deals go down and weighted bodies sink to anonymous graves. Like surly stevedores, the employees are ragged. Instead of those blue aprons, they wear whatever they please—which happens to be frayed, black clothing. The skin that's exposed on these sometimes brutish, sometimes waifish types is pale and covered in inky, green tattoos. The employees smoke cigarettes right at the front counter and they're always unhappy to see you. Unless, that is, you know 'em. Then they're especially unhappy, wishing you'd get a clue already and bug off. I love those guys!

When I get my food, the family platter that feeds four, I have to be careful cuz the floor's periodically slick with grease and sticky with spilled drinks. There's no air conditioning, so the windows are open; there are no screens, so flies are everywhere. There are ceiling fans – some of 'em even work! But only on the lowest setting, stirring the thick, greasy, smoky, humid air, somehow making it even hotter. The tables are made of the same black wood as the door, and addicts have hacked their initials, names, and wisdom into them.

And then imagine me, little old me, your humble narrator and main character, soon to be joined for the first time by Freddie Bessel, sitting in a corner, a shadowy corner, shadowier than any other corner, the shadowiest corner in the vilest Captain D's in the entire country, in the whole wide world, napkin on my lap, shaking a small paper envelope of sweetener (the kind that causes cancer) to put in my iced tea. A man in a booth nearby slumps to the floor of a grease overdose or maybe grease ecstasy. But I don't stop. Lit only by a heat-lamp that glares bright white cuz it's lost its red filter, imagine this drug montage in that movie house of your mind:

I sensuously pick up a piece of fried fish [FADE TO BLACK]. I sumptuously bite into the golden-brown breading [FADE TO BLACK]. I chew the fish [FADE TO BLACK]. Grease runs sexily down my hands [FADE TO BLACK]. Repeat again and again. Add some discordant guitar music for effect. At the end of the montage, I fall back, eyes glazed over in grease ecstasy, right as the guitars go wild and then fade themselves.

Think of the fat. The grease coursing through my veins. Hardening my arteries. Blood pressure rising. Oversized, flabby heart pumping blood faster and faster, working harder and harder to get the life essence through my narrowed passages. Arteriosclerosis heightening. Think of the distended stomach, my own version of tracks. I gain so much weight, a couple stairs winds me. But I keep going back. For more. Always for more. The boiling, churning oil. The scorching heat-lamps. They're my paraphernalia.

All of this adds up to seedy, lowdown, sordid.

True, I'm still a dwarf with stark white hair and a stark white beard. And I wear clean clothes of varying colors. And I live in an okay part of town. But what I lack in general squalor and depression, I make up for with enthusiasm for my malaise. And when I say enthusiasm, I mean a sullen disregard for everything; and that, in turn, fills me with enthusiasm (you know why).

After all, if there's one thing all drug noirs are about, it's finding a bit of pleasure in this grease-trap of a world. And a very little bit's all that can be found. For, and I say this with deepest gravity, we're all white dwarf stars that're burning out. We might as well be part of our own destruction …

Metaphorical, eh?

And that's when Freddie came in …

§ §

Freddie came in to Captain D's cuz the streets'd run dry. Not so much as a joint to be found, let alone any smack. I only know about one drug: grease. So, I bought him a hit of fried fish.

When he sat down, he took his sportscoat off in slow motion to accentuate his druggie cool. I asked how he did that, what with the slow motion and all. He shook his head, lit a cigarette, asked:

"What's your name?"

"Herbert Zerbert," I told him, nodding my head upwards to look smooth.

"So, HZ, how old are you?" He took a drag on his cigarette cuz that's what cool druggies do. Squares puff.

"43," I said.

"HZ-43, huh? Not bad."

I asked him his name and how old.

"You gonna finish that sentence? Can I get an 'are you?' for the end?"

I slowly shook my head. Freddie gave me his classic grin, which he later told me he'd patented.

"Well then, I'm Freddie. And I'm old."

"Old? Can't be. You're not even a Red Giant yet."

I knew Freddie was my man cuz he laughed like hell.

§ §

This is how well they know me: on the way out, stuffed so full of grease and fried animals my head swims along like the fish I consumed, they already have a to-go bag of hushpuppies waiting at the front. I love those guys! The crabby cashier holds my treasure in an apathetic hand, his other keeping his head from bouncing off the counter.

The manager knows me by name. I'm his best customer. Like a good dealer, the first time I came in, he gave me a coupon for a free meal. He hasn't given me a free meal since. What a guy!

§ §

Freddie and I talked all that night and into the morning, him yammering a mile a minute, his hands shaking. Around dawn, Freddie asked me what I was looking for.

"Same thing everyone else's looking for – a plot," I said.

Falling asleep, he mumbled: "Pot. We'll find some tomorrow."

§ §

The next day we were on the road to Nashville to score. Freddie had some contacts there, some guys looking to dump their stash and get out of the business. Tired of the heat.

And, anyway, a road-trip's essential to a good drug noir. Plenty of time for bonding between the mainman and his pal that sets you up for the inevitable downer ending, where everything that seemed cool and happy earlier, transforms into nostalgically depressing in a flourish of bittersweet perfection. I can't wait! Plus, with all the scenery whizzing by, there's gotta be a sign or a symbol that can recur. Look! There's one now:

An advertisement for Captain D's. It said: "Get Hooked On Us," and had a picture of a fishhook. So, from then on, whenever I was going to Captain D's, I'd make my finger into a hook and stick it in my mouth. Freddie'd do the same thing when he needed a hit. Nice. But we need a little more fish to fry.

The other convenient metaphor that appeared was a sign painted on a rundown barn. It said: "Millions have seen Rock City. Have you?"

"What's Rock City?" I asked.

"Huh?" said Freddie. He was preoccupied with the score.

"Have you ever been to Rock City?"

"Rock City?"

"Rock City."

Freddie gazed out the windshield. The air that arose during the conversational hiatus lent a sage-like quality to his answer. "No, man. I don't think I ever have." Then he added some dramatic repetition: "I don't think I ever have."

Another pause, this time to ponder how lines said twice, slowly, are just really cool.

"Have you, HZ-43?" he asked.

"No," I said. "No, I haven't."

"Who has?" he asked.

"Millions," I said.

"But not us."

§ §

Road-trips, like stories, have plot arcs. Drug noirs, they're the inverted Freytag. You think, hope the characters'll snap out of it, but they drop and drop until they hit bottom. Along the way, like looking out the window on a road-trip, things don't appear to be going in any particular direction. The route's crazy; that is, till you reach the destination. Then it all makes sense.

We were near one of those classically named cities, maybe

Carthage, Alexandria, or Athens, the flat part of our roadtrip, when Freddie asked me about life before Knoxville.

"First, I went in for the conventional squalor and drugs. I really did. I was so …! I mean—Got me an apartment in the absolute worst part of Memphis. But now, imagine me, little old me, four feet tall, big white beard, long white hair, in the ghetto. Doesn't really fit, huh? Maybe in a sideshow, but in the ghetto? No matter, I tried. Had an ancient, shabby couch (perfect for crashing on after drawn-out benders), filthy shag carpeting, walls whose stains were like poster-sized Rorschach Tests, rusty bars on the windows, exposed and banging pipes that leaked incessantly, neighbors who competed to see how loud they could make the other shout nonsense (day and night), and other neighbors who figured the only way to silence the screaming was to scream overtop of it. Between the window bars you could see the smokestacks of a factory that manufactured depression and dumped it in the river. When it rained, more water poured in from the ceiling than came out of the faucet. I had to wrestle the cockroaches. The rats ruled."

"Sounds like a pit," said Freddie.

"It was wonderful …! I mean, it was just right for a white dwarf who's slowly burning out …

"My first day in Memphis, I was raring to go. I hit the streets and scoped the place out. My neighborhood – a hellhole! It made me so happy ... And when I say 'happy,' of course I mean it depressed me in that drug ... Uh ... Nothing but dilapidated old buildings far as the eye could see. People carried guns around with impunity; they robbed passersby with the gusto of a grease-jockey cleaning the fry vats.

"I spied a guy hanging out on a street corner wearing a red shirt underneath a leather jacket. He moved in slow motion. He had a great big nose, a greasy mustache, and clunky glasses. I figured him for a dealer. He was standing on a corner, and that's where dealers stand."

Freddie laughed; I continued.

"'You carrying?' I asked, all smooth.

"'Hmm?' He looked down at me.

"'Got any blow?'

"'Blow?'

"'Or H?'

"'H ...? Is this some kind of joke? Who put that beard on you?'

"'What? It's my beard ... How about X? Come on, man. I need a high.'

"'Are you a dwarf?'

"'Yeah.'

"'A dwarf's trying to buy drugs from me. This is priceless. I gotta go tell Eddie.'

"'Hey, don't mess with me, man. I'm a junky. I'll do

anything for a score. Just look out, man.'

"'Or what? You'll hit me with your battle axe?'

"'I tell ya,' he said. 'Eddie's gonna love this.' And he wandered off."

Then we passed by the classically named city and left it behind us.

§ §

I've talked plenty. Now it's time for Freddie to give us some of his druggie mysticism.

At the end of my flashback, Freddie said:

"Do you ever think about stars?"

"Sure."

"You know how some stars go supernova, and some turn into neutron stars, some into pulsars, some into black dwarves and some into black holes?"

"Yeah."

"You ever wonder what it'd be like if the stars could think about where they were going? What would they want to be? What would they expect? Would they care about the other stars? Would they ever get confused?"

"I never thought about that."

"And if they did get confused, what would happen? How are they supposed to know what they're supposed to do?"

"I figure physics takes care of all that. They're stars. They really don't have any choices. Their lives are laid out for them whether they like it or not. Small stars will turn into dwarves; big stars will be supernovas, and maybe black holes."

Freddie paused, looking like he might even cry.

"Doesn't that seem really sad, man? I mean, doesn't it?"

§ §

At the deal. Easy. It's gonna go wrong.

It was in this house. Nothing too special about it. It wasn't in the ghetto, but it wasn't exactly in the best part of town either. Somewhere in between. Which is perfect cuz that messes up your idea of what a crackhouse is. And the five guys inside were all nervous cuz they were afraid we might be cops.

"What's with the dwarf?" one of them asked. The back of my neck began itching. Too much tension in the air. The dealers kept their hands behind them, probably where they had their guns.

"Yeah, you didn't say nothing about no dwarf," added another. One of the guys made like he was gonna leave the room. But Freddie stopped him.

"Fellas, I didn't realize I needed a license to carry one. Anyway, he's a friend."

"How do we know he won't snitch? How do *you* know?" they asked Freddie.

"Cuz I'm hooked, too," I said, making the fishhook to

Freddie.

"Hooked?! On what?"

"Grease," I said.

They relaxed and gave me a grave look, nodding their heads in unison as if I'd spoken the deepest line they'd ever heard. They were those kinds of guys. It was that kind of deal.

§ §

Don't worry. I really don't understand those last two sentences either. But they fit in a story like this. Trust me. They belong.

§ §

In the end, the deal went like a dream. The only way it could've turned out. Ya can't have the first deal be a bad deal. I know that …

§ §

No problem. I'm in control, on the path I've chosen for myself. Heck, even if I had a girlfriend as the second in my binary pair, I'd still continue on. A girlfriend. Think of that.

A beautiful blonde with a thing for dwarves sits facing me at Captain D's. The light slants across her face, revealing smeared mascara and tears. The ceiling fans are heard squeaking in the background. She barely contains her sobbing, while I devour fried fish by the dozens.

"I ... I ..."

"You got something to say, baby?" I ask, all cool like, my mouth full of batter. A fellow grease freak who weighs four hundred pounds hobbles in. I nod.

"I ... I just can't take it anymore! I can't stand by and watch you kill yourself like this!"

"You knew what I was like from the beginning, baby," I say, taking a big swig of sweetened iced tea out of the straw. "I haven't changed ... you have."

The blonde looks away from me, crestfallen, her beauty increasing with each new angle. How the heck did I end up with this girl?

"I know you haven't changed, Herbert. That's the thing. I thought I could change you." As she completes her sentence, I start eating two pieces of fish at the same time.

Chewing, speaking out of the side of my mouth, I say: "That's your problem, baby," pointing at her with a chicken plank as I swallow the fish. "Not mine."

"But I love you, Herbert. And I thought ..." she stops. I've made a chicken plank sandwich out of two chicken planks for the bread and a chicken plank center. "I thought you loved me." She watches me polish off the sandwich, then lay into the post-dinner hushpuppies. Unable to stand it anymore, she gets up in a huff and leaves.

"You'll be back!" I shout, showering myself with half-chewed breading. "You always come back!"

§ §

Sorry for the aside, but all we've missed is a traffic jam, which drags on and on. It feels like we'll never make it to our destination. To Knoxville.

Freddie said: "Ever notice, when traffic gets really bad, you start to think it'll never end. Like you'll be on this long, thin, depressing parking lot forever and ever. And then, if you're like me, you get to thinking, dreaming really, about the cars suddenly parting, moving aside, making a lane just for you. And when this groove opens, you drive by the rest of the cars, stunned, maybe stopping to wave to thank people, these kind souls who've selected you to be the one to move on, to represent them beyond the traffic jam; but soon you pick up more and more speed, until the other cars are a blur. And you get this idea that, when you pass by all the other folks, you'll feel so … superior, so satisfied that no heroin high could beat it. But that never happens. Instead, the cars all begin to move, you along with them, faster and faster, until the backup itself is lost in a drug-like haze. And you can't help but think that somehow you missed out on something."

And then the traffic did begin to move and we saw the

Rock City sign again, but on that side it only said, "See Rock City," and I got to thinking that Rock City was this amazing place where everyone went cuz it was so fulfilling, and you could stay as long as you wanted and everything you could possibly ever crave would be there and it would be the best stuff you ever had and all the people would be really cool and the whole experience would just blow you away cuz it couldn't get any better than life in Rock City, and that made me wonder how come I'd never heard of the place before if it's so flipping fantastic, which made me think that maybe Rock City didn't exist and the guy who painted all those signs was trying to get us to think about something happy while we were driving on the highway and it was a kind of metaphysical challenge to See Rock City since there wasn't any such place, or maybe the guy was a bastard, so it was a taunt, "Sure, See Rock City, if you can," and man this has to be one of them defining stream-of-consciousness moments where the main character displays a balls-out yearning for something completely abstract, only he channels it through something concrete which leads to an absolute letdown, that inevitable downer ending. And let me tell you, that ending, I can't wait till we get there. I love them things.

§ §

Back in K-town.

It's salad days. Which is a good thing, I guess. Ya ask me, it ought to be "fried fish days." That would be better than salad. Sheesh.

Freddie had a house and a band of followers. Cuz of the drugs. I'd bring my hushpuppies, and as folks plunged needles into their veins, or snorted dust, or dropped paper squares, or smoked, or huffed, or drank, or ate laced brownies, I'd suck down my greaseballs, hot as can be.

"I'm the Everyjunky," sez Freddie, bright red shirt blazing from underneath his otherwise black clothes. "I do all the drugs and I know what it's like to be any one of you. I know that coke binge that lasts days, sometimes weeks, mind racing. And I know the H dreams, the prophetic visions. I know the euphoria of E. I know the buck wild invincibility of PCP. I know the drunken lost weekends. I know the mind-altering madness of acid. And I know the crystal clarity of crystal meth. Yes, I've taken uppers, downers, screamers, laughers. I've stumbled through forgotten buildings on ether, and seen the slanted world of mescaline. And I am here to tell you, I understand each and every one of my children. I even understand my little friend, HZ-43's fix."

Freddie, patting me on the head, continued walking through the crowd, weaving his way around.

If you couldn't tell, this is where I let Freddie do most of the talking to better flesh out his character.

"And do you know what I've come to understand? We're standing on a dimensional borderline. On one side is that which we know but despise, on the other is what we don't know and are afraid of. We don't want to go back to the land we despise, but we're not ready to enter the land we fear. So, we remain on the borderline, staring towards the red undiscovered country."

Freddie paused, sauntering through the crowd, red shirt shining, his consciousness expanding, perhaps invading and encompassing that of every druggie.

"But do not stare too deeply into that country beyond. For beyond is the apocalypse. And although it appears to be light years away, it'll come for us. It will distend in our direction. And if you stare forever at the expanding apocalypse, you'll end up as fried as my little friend's fish dinners. Isn't that right HZ-43?"

Then, just to me, he crouched down, eyes glazed, focused as if they weren't looking at me but seeing some strange and fantastic vision, and asked, "So, how does that speech fit into your story?"

Back at Captain D's I'd sit in my shadowiest corner and think about Freddie's speeches, sometimes with one or more of the other addicts, overly bright heat-lamp shining on my white hair. We were all the same. We were all burning out. We all knew it. We all accepted it. We were all white dwarf stars waiting for the needle to hit empty. Knowing it would run out. Daring it to run out. And it always runs out. Believe me.

§ §

Everything's back on track, since I only made one mistake.

"I hate this town," a girl on the front lawn said. She wore a green bikini, comically large sunglasses, and a basket-of-fruit hat. She was coming down, and anytime a druggie comes down, they hate their towns. The hangover's gotta be someone's fault. Might as well blame the city. Plus, random, unnamed yet slightly described characters give the protagonist a chance to perform. Warms the readers up to him.

"What's wrong with Knoxville?" I asked, smiling.

"It's just all fucked up, man. It's just all fucked up." Was the dramatic repetition done purposefully? I don't know. But life could always use a good dose of dramatic repetition.

"Could you be more specific?"

"You be more Pacific. I'm from Knoxville, man, so lay off."

"All right. It sounds like you like Knoxville," I said.

"I hate this fucking town. It's the worst. I mean, look what they did to the Sunsphere."

In the distance, the Sunsphere was being refurbished. It'd been under construction for like five years. It was never going to be completed. The money ran out. While under construction, it was white instead of gold cuz it was covered with tarps.

"Don't think of it like that. Think of it as the Sunsphere's last hurrah. It's had a long, rather rough life, so now it's burning twice as bright as before. Even if it's smaller. Don't give up until it turns black. Cuz then it'll never shine again."

Pause.

"Anyway," I said, "I think the Sunsphere's a binary pair. Maybe its companion burns brighter."

"A ... A *what*? Where's the other one?"

"Have you ever been to Rock City?"

"Um, yeah, like when I was a kid ..."

There's an awkward silence.

"Trippy, man," she said. "Are you, like, a dwarf?"

"Yeah, but I used to be a giant."

"What happened?"

"Ran out of energy, shrunk way down."

"I never met a giant before."

I gave a sighing, pregnant pause and said: "And I've never been to Rock City."

Then I ate a hushpuppy.

§ §

The oil churns around my fish and the white heatlamp

blazes. It's time to get my order to go cuz, oboy, oboy, it's time for the unavoidable mass arrest. No question, the cops'll roar up, sirens blaring, lights flashing, bullhorns wailing, guns cocking, druggies scattering. We'll be taken to jail for possession, distribution, association. It'll be great! And then later we'll get out just in time for the inevitable downer ending.

But let's enjoy the stages as they come along.

At the house, the party continued as per normal. Think of Bosch's *The Garden of Earthly Delights* and add drug paraphernalia and you pretty much get the idea. I sat down on the front porch, smiling, and began to wait for the police cars, eating my fried everything.

"Hey, HZ-43. How's it going?" Freddie asked, white shirt on underneath his black clothes. He's smoking something or other, so he's surrounded by a green mist.

I made the fishhook and Freddie laughed, nodding knowingly.

"Whatcha doin'?"

"Waitin' for the cops to show up. Should be here any minute," I said, mouth stuffed full of fries.

Freddie said: "What do you mean?" But he spoke with sarcastic exaggeration.

"This party's gone on so long, how could they not find out about it?"

"Ah, you're paranoid."

"Nope. Just know how these things work. It's the time in the story when the cops show up …"

"Well, you're in control, HZ."

"… and they should be here right about," and I point behind me.

"Oh shit!" screamed Freddie, so loud even I turned around. But nothing's there.

I'm speechless.

Freddie, all-knowing look on his face, white shirt shining in the sun, smiled.

"Oh, they'll be here, Freddie. You wait and see. They might be here already, undercover, eager to pounce. *Just you wait.*"

"I bet you a trip to Rock City they don't show up."

"You're on."

"So if they show up, we go to Rock City on your terms (if we can get out of jail). If they don't, we go to Rock City on mine."

Something seemed off about the bet, but I took it. Then I stared at the street, willing the cops to appear, the silence going on forever.

"HZ-43, you know why paranoids trap themselves up in their rooms?"

"Sure, Freddie. So the people who are after 'em don't take

'em away."

"No. That's the cover. Paranoids stay in their rooms because otherwise they'd have to come face to face with the overwhelming evidence that disproves their claims."

Smiling, leaning back in my chair, legs dangling, swinging below me, I waited for the cops. Thinking, any minute now the five-oh will appear. Which is fine with me. I'm ready. It's in the script. I only hope I get to finish my Captain D's before they take me downtown.

All that night me and Freddie sat on the porch, staring at the road, waiting for the fuzz, waiting for the evidence that'd prove I wasn't paranoid, that'd prove I knew exactly where this story was going, a trip to Rock City hanging in the balance.

But no one ever came.

§ §

Somewhere during the course of the night, I fell asleep. I dreamed about a time when I was a kid and my mom took me to a store that had a standup version of *Asteroids* and my mom wouldn't let me have a quarter to play. But I played anyway by pretending that I was in control during the demo cycle. Each time the little ship moved, I thought to myself that I made it move that way. And each time it shot an asteroid, I said that I shot the asteroid. And when the ship finally wrecked, signaling its demise, I accepted that demise as my own.

§ §

The next morning the sun woke me up. I figure, since the cops never showed, now it's time for all the drugs to run out and for all the addicts to leave. Then it'll be me and Freddie all by our lonesome and we'll talk about stuff and wish we had whatever.

But Freddie's gone. No one knew where he was. Nobody cared. And the party continued.

I don't know *what* part of the story this is.

Maybe this is the part where Freddie goes off on a bender by himself, out of his mind on any combination of drugs, ending up in a flophouse somewhere and I'm the only one who can find him, who can talk some sense into him, who can teach him the importance of ... something important. Maybe this is the part where Freddie disappears cuz, although the cops never showed, he got freaked out and figured they would, and they'd pin it all on him. Maybe this is the part where Freddie and I have a falling out cuz ... cuz we're both so toasted we get in a completely irrational argument that can only be understood by other junkies. Maybe this is the part where Freddie goes straight and when I see him again he'll be at one of those Southern revivals where everyone gets saved and healed. Maybe this is the part where we learn that Freddie was actually a cop, but couldn't bring himself to arrest all the druggies cuz they're just people looking to make their lives worthwhile. Maybe this is the part where we find out that Freddie never existed, he was actually a construct of the narrator, a person who represented what the narrator wished he was ... but how can Freddie be that? I mean, he's barely been in the story ... Maybe ... Maybe ... Or maybe this is the part where I walk around town and feel sorry for myself cuz nothing turned out the way I wanted, nothing became dark and sordid and noirish. Hell, the varying tenses weren't even that confusing. But it'll be all right, for me, anyway, if I look up and find I'm in the absolute worst part of the city, the part you don't go into unless you're connected, the part you stay out of unless you're backed by an army, the part you're warned about, and nobody will bother me cuz I fit in so well, too well, with all their pain.

The normalcy of the neighborhood is appalling. There's no underworld romance here. No noir atmosphere. No wise homeless folks, deteriorated buildings, aimless potholed streets, blind alleys, graffiti. There are no flashy pimps, dirty whores, bagladies, winos. Here we have people and houses and lawns and plants and cement and asphalt and quaint and safe and boring.

I walk to my Captain D's to get a hit. The door won't open. There's a sign in the window. It's from the Knoxville Health Department. It addresses me directly. It really does. It sez:

Dear Herbert Zerbert,

This is the part of the story where you realize there never was a Captain D's like you've described. This is the part of the story where you realize so many things are not how you described them. This is the part of the story where you must address your obsession with burning out. This is the part of the story where you must face reality. This is the part of the story where you sit down on a stoop and think about your life.

Sincerely,
K.H.D.

So, I guess this is the part of the story where I sit on a stoop and think about my life. I could give a damn what part of the story this is. I don't know anything about this story, anyway. I wonder who does. So, I just stand and stare at the ground. After a while, a hand falls on my shoulder.

"We found Freddie."

§ §

If this is even remotely the story I think it is, it's time for me to go into a metaphorical, dreamlike offshoot that, while heightening the suspense as to what happened to Freddie, ties everything together. All the motifs, characters, metaphors … all the yearning. What better place for it to be set than in Rock City? *My* Rock City.

No such luck. I'm not in control anymore. Maybe I never was. So, I'm in the real Rock City. It's not so bad. There are rocks. There's a path through the rocks. For whatever reason, there are little gnomes setup throughout the rock formations. There are caves. There's a trippy section where fairy tale scenes painted with black-light paint are displayed in the caves, amongst the rocks. There's an animatronic gnome who sits at the front and sings, "Big Rock Candy Mountain." "Big Rock Candy Mountain" would be a good song for this story, since its lyrics and tone parallel ... But I lack the hydrogen. It's all gone. There's a place where you look out from a cliff and supposedly see five different states. They all look pretty much the same. There's a rope bridge. A stone bridge. The whole tour costs like $15. It's a tourist trap.

And all throughout, even though you're already there, signs read: "See Rock City."

If you ask me, they forgot a comma. It should be pronounced in a deadpan: "See, Rock City."

I sit down on a bench at the end. At the end of Rock City. At the end of this story. Freddie sits next to me. Finally, he wears all black. All black.

"Still have enough energy for some dramatic repetition, huh?"

"Yeah."

"Cheer you up any?"

"Nah."

"What's wrong, little buddy?"

"Things didn't go how I expected. How I wanted. Never found a plot."

"You weren't in the right kind of story."

"What kind of story was I in?"

"I should know – it was a satire. You see, you thought we were on similar paths. But actually, I was a supergiant. And now I'm a black hole."

I feel myself getting sucked in by Freddie.

"How should you …?" I begin to ask, but then I think about it. The drug deal that went really well, the cops never showing up, the party never clearing out, no one ever dying, and the guy who wouldn't sell me drugs in Memphis, who set me off on this satirical path, was wearing a pathetic disguise (that I fell for)—and he *moved in slow motion*. Freddie was in control the entire time! Just like in the best drug noirs, I'd lost control!

My fatal flaw – I forgot about red shift!

My joy doesn't last long. Cuz I think about the note from the KHD. If I never met Freddie at Captain D's, since my Captain D's didn't exist, then that only leaves little old me.

"Well, you can't say I didn't try," sez Freddie.

"Yeah."

"What's wrong now?"

"Things didn't turn out the way I wanted."

"Do things ever turn out alright in this kinda story?"

"That's …" I stop. He's right. These are his terms. Freddie made sure the story ended properly.

"I'm sorry I didn't get to know you better, Freddie."

"It's cool, HZ-43. I'm only a character. Words on a page. You don't owe me anything. It's been fun being the enigmatic center. Thanks for bringing me along."

"Sure," and I give a grin. Freddie shoots his classic smile. US Patent Number … Whatever.

"See. And look around you."

Although we're still in Rock City, somehow we're also in my squalid Captain D's. And everything's as it should be. All the partiers are there. And the Rock City outside is the one I wanted. And the only light that shines in our direction is the heat-lamp. But I can't get into the whole scene.

"I guess this is goodbye, Freddie."

"I thought you were looking forward to the big, inevitable downer ending."

"Guess it's not what I expected it would be." Then I make the fishhook motion. Freddie laughs like hell.

"So you never were addicted to fried fish, right? You were addicted to drug noirs."

I pause to let the tension build.

"I'm not an addict. I can quit whenever I want."

The heat-lamp fizzles out. Freddie, in all black, is now lit only by his cigarette. Then he extinguishes it and I never see him again.

I get up on my short legs and walk to the door of the Captain D's. Everything begins disappearing around me. I don't know exactly what kind of story this is, but if it's the story I want it to be the guy at the counter will stop me with a bag of hushpuppies. The manager'll be with him. There in the increasing vacuum of space.

"Few hushpuppies to go?" he'll ask, shaking the bag.

"Not this time."

"Come on, they're on the house," sez the manager. What a guy. Then he disappears. And the crabby cashier, as if it's the most annoying task in the world, finally disappears, too. Leaving only this white dwarf, little old me, in the expanding nothing.

But this is the inevitable downer ending that you saw coming a mile away, so I just keep walking, through the disappearing lobby. Out the door. My light getting dimmer and dimmer, illuminating my hair and beard one last time. And then into the darkness.

That is, if this is that kind of story.

I Don't Know Why

"no symbols where none intended"
- Samuel Beckett
Watt

The Heat Death of the Universe

You will think, & maybe you're right, you can't ever tell, that this sounds like an end, the end, the end of a story, not the beginning, not a commencement, full of possibility, of probability, where the readers start w/ so much, so much, & look forward, w/ great anticipation, to the conclusion, the denouement, where the possibilities are brought to one, probability fulfilled, beginning, middle, & the beautiful end, winding through, again & again, like a ratchet & gear, a simple machine, an almost perfect machine, leaving nothing to chance, or very little to chance, randomness being so unsatisfying, the story must be about someone, must go somewhere, must resolve all conflict, must have closure; you will think this, there in the future, when, w/r/t my project, viz. Knoxville project, i.e. Sunsphere stories, the Sunsphere showing up throughout, in various forms, I tell you I am now on the entropy story, the penultimate story (so fancy for 2nd to last), before final stasis, that end, brings the spinning, pulsing work to a full stop, & I tell you, all I have is an image, of Knoxville, fantasy Knoxville (of course), wherein the city has grown chaotic, utter chaos, sprawling this way, that way, every which way, has expanded & expanded "in all of the directions it can whiz" (Monty Python reference), but it has now stopped, will stop, there in the future, & w/ it my ideas have stopped; you will recall, I know you will, I claimed to have many, many ideas w/r/t the project, but that's not the truth, not at all, instead I have fragments of ideas, or fragments of fragments, none of which will come together, none of which will take us to that ending, oh that ending, so far away, perhaps illusory, for now there is only an image, a prospect, of a town w/o business, w/o industry, that resembles, what? Godzilla's Tokyo (what an awful idea), or actually, a fantasy Tokyo (of course), or a fantasy Godzilla's Tokyo (what an awful idea (of course)) where the Godzilla-style monsters, so monstrous, have all attacked, not like the movies, not at all, where it seems as if, to me anyhow, that the attacks have occurred in parallel dimensions, the city in one piece, & nobody remembering what it was like last time, & surely they would recall, all too well, if a Tyrannosaurus rex came along, out of nowhere, & destroyed their city, but no, no one remembers, not an inkling, not a sliver of light, so, ∴, the attack must never have happened, never before, but in this case, in this one case, imagine a Tokyo attacked by Anguirus,

Baragon, Biollante, Destroyah, Ebirah, Gabara, Gamera, Gigan, Godzilla, Gorgo, Gorosaurus, Guidra, Hedorah, Jet-Jaguar, Kamacuras, King Caesar, King Ghidorah, King Kong, Kumonga, Manda, Mechagodzilla, Mecha-King Ghidorah, Megaguirus, Megalon, Minilla, Mogera, Monster X, Monster Zero, Mothra, Orga, Rodan, Space Godzilla, Titanosaurus, & Varan, & any other monsters, any others I may be leaving out, imagine they attacked & fought in this fantasy Tokyo every time, there in the future, the Japanese, of course, would have to rebuild, reconstruct their fair city after each attack &/or battle, meaning (oh this vision) they would likely start, before the 1st Godzilla invasion, w/ Tokyo, then after, rampage, destruction, would have to rebuild, leaving them w/ Old Tokyo (the part devastated by Godzilla) & New Tokyo (the city created in Godzilla's wake, possibly by those, full of greed, wishing to capitalize on public funds, the SPQR), & then, soon after completion, Godzilla returns, from the deep blue sea, & fights Mothra or Rodan or Mechagodzilla, a battle which would leave in its wake Old Old Tokyo, Old New Tokyo, & New New Tokyo, & then, yet again, the monsters would disappear, & then return, & fight, & rampage, & leave, forming Old Old Old Tokyo, Old Old New Tokyo, Old New New Tokyo, & New New New Tokyo, on into ∞, forever & ever, which is what will happen, there in the future, to Knoxville, only in place of monster attacks, not very likely, there will be revitalization programs, forming labyrinthine neighborhoods, grids no longer popular, cul-de-sac supremacy, until twisting, turning enclaves wrap in on themselves (every street having c. five names (names fluctuating willy-nilly), dead-ending into other streets, randomly beginning elsewhere, wherever that is), stranding the inhabitants, the hapless folks who often can't recall how they ended up in Knoxville, if they know where they live at all, completely lost, surrounded by flies, where can the garbage be taken? cut off from each other, the citizens no longer even speak the same language, isolation, so dialects have arisen, some complicated, some only accents, the city, there in the future, might as well be full of static, white noise, b/c of the impossibility of communication, & gone is the Sunsphere, that big, golden microphone, World's Fair Park's vacant, a star's burned out, & nobody cares, & nothing happens, the people don't move, where would they go? nothing gets done, what is there to do? there is no possibility of work, how can heat be transferred? you will think that sounds like an ending, & not *the* ending, the ending where everything will be explained, where all loose ends will be tied, where satisfaction will be gained, where order will be restored, where you will be happy to lose yourself in the main character (there are no characters), where you will be the main character (equally impossible w/o characters), yes, you will think that sounds like an ending, but no, it is not, not an ending, a beginning, possibly the beginning of the end, maybe the collection, the project, viz. Knoxville project, i.e. Sunsphere stories, will never be completed, for I can't see where it will go, this story, entropy story, how it will move past, way past, this stagnation, & it must to reach completion, that conclusion, denouement, that will explain all, it's the end of a world that's hardly begun, there in the future. & P.S., my air conditioner just went out. So, it's 90° in here. I should know. I took a thermometer & checked every room in the house. They're all the same.

The Quasi-Steady State Theory

Sez you, futurewise, don't you worry about the ending b/c maybe this vehicle you got here is an episodic creation that always appears to end, always seems to reach its conclusion, that final thrust before the darkness ... but oh no, here we go again, another fork in the road, another Freytag in the road saying he wants a ride up that great big hill in the distance a- & we only thought this was the conclusion b/c everything's leveled out, when it turns out that each leveling out is the ground situation for another trip up that rollercoaster hill, a- &, hell, this time we might take off into outer space, ship controlled by a photon drive that runs on the blueshift to redshift cosmic background radiation (CBR) meaning we don't ever need any propellant a-& our only limit will be the limits of the universe, but even there, just when we think we've come to the end of the matter, bang! more matter's created, more universe, a whole new part that didn't even exist before, a-& there in the Great Grand Opening will be a fork in the vacuum, a Freytag in the vacuum saying ... yeah, but for now, sez you, futurewise, we need a character to follow, someone we can cheer for, someone who can bear our hopes, dreams, fears, someone who can help direct our emotions, possibly someone who's ≈ us, someone who'll be a shining beacon, a cynosure in our night sky we can lock our instruments onto a-& that way we'll know where we're going, if there's gonna be chaos let's have a guy who strives for order, a guy, when he's a kid, e.g., who'll be bored a-& intelligent, so he's self-conscious, a-& then in his late teens/early twenties becomes a confident intellectual, a-& then in his later twenties a less confident intellectual, a questioner, a rationalizer, a-& then he marries, living happily for a while, then the marriage goes sour, life likewise, a-& then he stops being married, stops doing whatever it is he does, sez me, he's an expediter, he's called the Expediter, sez you, futurewise, repeating my exact thoughts back to me, yeah, well he goes on to become a physics professor b/c he picked up some physics degrees years ago, but thought he should work for the gov. instead for the good of the people (maybe even AMDG), a-& he's an absentminded professor who goes on these rants that get him the name the Prophet of Science, a-& then he has a stroke, a-& then [blank], a-& then death; well, man, that's what you're gonna say, a-& I won't stop you, seeing as how you're saying exactly, *exactly* what I'm thinking, so, sez you, a-& what I'm thinking is you need a purpose for those Knoxvillians, they're gonna start building a wall, like the Great Wall of China, around their city, a-& they're going to build a wall b/c the Mayor told them to over the speakers (a-& when the SPQR speaks, people listen), but wait, that's way out there in the Æther, so let's back this ship up a bit, a-& what we've got is this depressed city from last time, well they finally get to noticing that the Sunsphere's missing, wondering how the Mayor could let such a thing happen, what kind of mayor would do that? wait a minute, just *who is the Mayor?* there's gotta be a mayor, right? but the people won't know if there's a mayor or not, certainly no one can remember electing a mayor, it's like one year the entire election process slipped their minds, a-& by "their" I mean everyone's minds, the old mayor stepping down, but nobody running to replace him, so there are phantom candidates, who run imaginary campaigns, that lead to an unheard of lack of controversy, culminating in a fiercely nonexistent debate won by no one, a-& all that's on anyone's mind, all that anyone's talking about is anything but an election, a-& finally, after the mud that wasn't slung has settled, the big day rolls around a-& the pollsters, unconsciously, make sure there are no pens, pencils unsharpened, voter registration sheets unprinted, ballots neither confusing nor clear, halls for voting not secured, lights turned off, signs indicating where the un-election is taking place nowhere to be found, the constituents staying home in droves, nothing to report on the news, a-&, in the end, the un-campaigns lead to an un-election of no one at all; but what's a town w/o a mayor? no, there's gotta be a mayor, somewhere, one day the Knoxvillians just went on w/ their lives a-& figured the Mayor went on w/ his or hers, a-& it's thinking like this that leads to the speakers being put up, sez you, futurewise, my own puppet, no one knowing where the speakers came from, but everyone, or just about, knowing that the speakers connect them to the Mayor, their very own Freytag, a-& one day those very same speakers will broadcast a catalyzing message, a message that'll give the Knoxvillians a purpose, that'll bring everything back to order b/c that's what mayors do, especially this mayor, whoever he or she might be ... well, as it turns out, the people will finally be contacted by the Mayor, or at least it'll be rumored that they've been rewarded w/ a speech, though no one will be certain b/c some of the speakers, by this time, futurewise, will be broken, a-& some aren't technically connected to anything, a-& what w/ the various dialects not all the words have the same meanings to one group as compared to another, so some will never hear the Mayor say a single word, while others'll claim that the Mayor's been speaking to them for years, a-& others will claim one message, while another group'll claim another, a-& then some think it's some kind of hoax put on by the KnoxVillains (but who are they? I'll get there in a second), a-& some think there's no message at all, but in the end a general message will be constructed piecemeal-style, jury-rigged, slapped together higgledy-piggledy, although the sender won't be known for certain, but the people will believe the Mayor has told them to build a wall a-& to banish the KnoxVillains, a gang of malcontents who kidnapped the Sunsphere, deconstructed it, reconstructed it, a-& returned it to World's Fair Park, a giant glass ziggurat, since, futurewise, sez you, futurewise, the KnoxVillains took all the Sunsphere pieces, placed them in glass blocks, set the glass blocks up in World's Fair Park, w/ the Sunsphere out of order inside the ziggurat, a-& now any other chaos or mischief that takes place in Knoxville is blamed on the KnoxVillains, so the wall is to be built so the KnoxVillains can be banished, a-& if the Knoxvillians will build this wall a-& banish the KnoxVillains, then order will be restored, only that part about order being restored doesn't come from the Mayor per se, it'll come from the Knoxvillians who immediately start inventing reasons to build a wall b/c they believe in the Mayor a-& they figure the Mayor has their best interests in mind whenever s/he broadcasts a plan, a-& since there's currently chaos, futurewise, it just stands to reason that there'll be order once the wall is built, not to mention jobs, prosperity, a chicken in every pot, a car in every garage, a-& on a-& on, the people will come up w/ plenty of reasons to build the wall, plenty of positive outcomes from the wall, but, uh, oh yeah, no actual *ways to build the wall*, a-& to symbolize this absurdity I'm thinking there should be, like, a children's song, either "There Was an Old Woman Who Swallowed a Fly" or "There's a Hole in the Bottom of the Sea," since both of those songs are utterly ludicrous, a-& I think they fit in w/ the ideas of chaos a-& entropy working here, sez you, futurewise, but w/ this much material there'll be beginnings – middles – a-& ends w/o end, so don't you worry about the end of the story; and I won't. I'm not even worried about the air conditioner. The repairman's coming tomorrow. As it turns out, my air conditioner's in my basement. Here I didn't even know I had a basement.

The Steady State Theory (or The Infinite Universe Theory)

N.B.: to illustrate the physical state of Knoxville being represented by this author, although not a prerequisite to visitation, you will construct a scale model of the conurbation, proving, unnecessarily, for said knowledge will have already been acquired, that the cessation of the tale is not the crux, indeed, the commencement is, for the conclusion will transpire naturally, will be enlightening, will satisfy the mental faculties put into machination by the question posed at the outset; the antiphon to the aforementioned conundrum w/r/t the genesis of this municipality is that Knoxville, as clearly as the night sky is dark although the stars are infinite, has always been the same, has never undergone a single metamorphosis, has only appeared to do so speciously b/c the inhabitants themselves have grown dissolute, said dissolution metastasizing in the form of the KnoxVillains, a&a the only solution to this dilemma is to strive for the inherent order that is still, a&a always has been extant; for it is not the expansion of Knoxville that is the bugbear, for Knoxville has forever been expanding, it is the cognizance of ibid by the citizenry; the act of building the wall, then, is symbolic for, being ∞, everything that can happen, will happen, or, more precisely, has already happened in Knoxville, it is ∴ a matter of adjusting perception to reality which the people of Knoxville believe will occur when they finish their wall; to portray this apparent but not actual fluctuation in time a&a space, this author will utilize a series of narrators, all of whom will be tonally differentiated, all of whom will narrate one section of $\approx$ length, all of whom will represent a contrary position in the tale symbolizing the difficulty of clarifying perception when one's experience opposes the new data; the story itself will progress telescopically from the Expediter (i.e., one citizen in Knoxville), to the gov. (i.e., the controlling body of Knoxville), to the metropolis itself, similar to Dr. Freud's superego, ego, a&a id respectively, for the Expediter shall be moral a&a industrious, contrary to the prosaic theories concerning civil servants; it has come, will come (for they are the same) to this author's attention that the literature at hand is similar to Herr Kafka's "The Great Wall of China" a&a Señor Borges' "The Wall a&a the Books," so contrasts a&a comparisons shall be made; w/r/t the Kafka, wherein the Chinese often meditate on the composition of the office of the command (their own SPQR), cf. this author's piece where the citizenry forget about the Mayor for an extended period, in the Kafka the narrator believes that the high command has always existed as did the decision to build the wall, cf. this author's piece where the orderly Knoxville has always existed a&a the wall is an expedient to get to that place, in the Kafka the laborers deem the method of piecemeal construction wise, cf. this author's tale where the workers formulate reasons for a wall to be erected w/o also concocting modes in which to build the wall proper, hence leading to the general collapse of portions of the wall, in turn forcing the laborers to reconstruct ibid, should they recall where they were employed the day previous, for the expanding (perceived) labyrinth compels the majority of the workforce, upon arising @ daybreak, to amble in a random direction until said mechanics et. al discover a portion of the wall, conducting their operation on this arbitrarily selected area, ∴ leading to segments being worked upon by legions of laborers a&a architects, utterly superfluous a&a ∴ in tune w/ the civil servant theories, three persons doing the job of one, meaning two of the aforementioned persons will be consuming caffeinated beverages or talking lewdly about lewd goings-on, whilst other sections of the wall shall be frightfully undermanned, including dilapidated fragments in dire need of care, in brief, this operation not being so nearly efficient a&a ingenious as the building of Herr Kafka's wall, "a&a for that reason I shall not proceed any further @ this stage w/ my inquiry into these questions;" w/r/t the Borges, this author has as of yet not devised any parallels btw his own piece a&a Señor Borges' "The Wall a&a the Books," for Borges' article about Shih Huang Ti, the emperor who both declared the imminent construction of the Great Wall of China a&a confined all tomes written before his reign to perdition, said tale concerns a personage who perceives himself as the center of the universe, a&a since the Expediter is no such individual, a&a since the Mayor will only "appear" via his/her speakers a&a/or the rumor mill (viz., i.a.), his transmissions becoming more abstruse b/c, subsequent to his original broadcast, all of the speakers in Knoxville, of which there will be millions (a&a, N.B., each will be painstakingly represented in your model), indeed, all of the speakers will relay static, the static building in puissance, from the sound of snow, to drizzling rain, to pounding precipitation, until it drowns all else out, the citizenry believing that perhaps the Mayor is punishing them for not erecting the wall in a more rapid fashion, for not banishing the KnoxVillains fast enough, which justifies why the Knoxvillians do not wreak havoc upon said speakers, for the civilians also believe that the Mayor will speak unto them in a loud, clear voice once the grand civic beautification project has been brought to a firm conclusion, once the KnoxVillain threat is dealt w/, a&a then the true reality of Knoxville will shine through, although, in opposition to this view, there are those who give credence to the prognosis that the KnoxVillains are to blame for the static, a&a that once these miscreants are handled in an appropriate fashion, the inhabitants of the then walled city will again be in direct contact w/ the Mayor, but since, much like the Expediter, the Mayor is not to be taken as a Shih Huang Ti, how the Borges will work in the text, this author does not know @ this time, unless it is that the people come to believe "that immortality is intrinsic a&a that decay cannot enter a closed orb;" what this author does know, however, is that the juvenile song "There Was an Old Woman Who Swallowed a Fly" will be utilized:

> There was an old woman who swallowed a fly,
> I don't know why she swallowed a fly,

Perhaps she'll die,

for this song expresses a philosophy of life which states that life is chaos, ∴ human beings are generated randomly (There was an old woman), defined randomly (for there would be no elderly female w/o the airborne insect), live lives of ignorance (I don't know why) a&a absurdity (the act of ingesting the fly) w/ the lone guarantee being that they will perish, but at a random time, a&a furthermore, when the inhabitants of Knoxville awaken from their dissolution to the light of reality, they will perceive that their situation was as absurd as a woman swallowing a goat in order to arrest a dog, a&a, indeed, the only conclusion the Knoxvillians will be able to hit upon will be, "I don't know why …" a&a, as a quick addendum, yet another symbol to be exploited in this tale will be the microphone, the Sunsphere, prior to its being transformed into a ziggurat, resembling a microphone, the Expediter speaking into a microphone he believes to be connected to nothing, the Mayor's microphone, etc. etc.; indeed, the general (perceived) chaos of Knoxville is all skillfully wrought in your (apologies, unnecessary) model depicting the ∞ metropolis whose beginning is unheard of, for the city has always been there, but whose ending can only lead to a superb enlightenment—AMDG. a&a, once again, this author's air conditioning is operational. It is nice a&a cool. Although, outside, it sounds like rain.

The Big Rip

… ~&~ you'll probably think I've gone too far or say I should take a break or you'll try to Δ your model in such a way that will convince me to slow down but I don't have time to dwell on the answer b/c I've now decided (as I feel possessed by a phantom energy which will certainly transform the conclusion of the story into one of those blasted open-ended ellipsis pieces) that the story will move beyond its previous borders into the realm of metafiction yet this metafiction will out-meta metafiction – the opening line being "I'm an unreliable metanarrator – no – that's a lie – I'm not unreliable – I'm not a metanarrator" ~&~ whereas before everything was coherently contained in the telescopic movement I no longer believe that that's fit for the subject matter so everything will be fragmented – having hit on this idea b/c I continue to come up w/ ideas @ an exponentially increasing rate when before I couldn't come up w/ any ideas @ all w/r/t the project so as the material itself begins to tear I've now decided that there'll be 8 macro sections as there are in "There Was an Old Woman" each macro section containing 3 micro sections b/c of the macro/micro ideas inherent in entropy ~&~ each micro section will be entitled Beginning ~&~ Middle ~&~ End to play w/ the idea of Freytag's Triangle ~&~ the obsession w/ the classic story formula each macro having an increasing # of ubermeta sections (similar to the beginnings of each book in Henry Fielding's *Tom Jones*) wherein the narrator for that macro (for there will be 8 different narrators) will deal w/ various meta concepts explaining both the tactics ~&~ the metatactics being used in the story since by now those metatactics are just as traditional as the previous tactics that were meta-ed (if not more so) ~&~ those ubermeta sections will be entitled Beginning of the Beginning ~&~ Beginning of the Middle ~&~ Beginning of the End ~&~ Middle of the Beginning ~&~ Middle of the Middle ~&~ Middle of the End ~&~ End of the Beginning ~&~ End of the Middle ~&~ End of the End ~&~ the story will progress like "There Was an Old Woman" in that it will start w/ relative absurdity working all the way up to complete absurdity for I feel that in this world gravity is just as likely to stop working as continue so everything must be shredded …

Beginning	*Middle*	*End*
… b/c the Knoxvillians now focus only on their wall although the focus is skewed – the focus itself is out of focus for they are not able to step back ~&~ observe the project from the outside ~&~ so they're not able to	… b/c the Expediter (being a good civil servant (contrary to the stereotype)) works all this time (even coming in early to do his speaking into the microphone he thinks isn't connected to anything routine) to	… b/c a professor speaks elaborately into a microphone about the end of the universe – explaining the various theories on what might happen – 1st talking about the Steady State Theory (or the ∞ Universe Theory) wherein there was no

205

completely understand what's going on – their city flying into chaos what w/ the KnoxVillains continuing to cause havoc by adding onto the city faster ~&~ faster making it more ~&~ more difficult to know where to put the wall – so w/ the city always expanding even the sections of the wall that are beautifully planned – beautifully constructed ~&~ beautifully completed – well it's all only beautiful if you don't take into account the fact that the stunning fragment being observed is only about one hundred yards long ~&~ appears to be – no it actually is right smack in the middle of a neighborhood ~&~ not on the outside of the city where a make things operate better by guarding against the coming of a character named the Horseman who is rumored to be the scariest member of the KnoxVillains b/c whereas the other KnoxVillains are agents of discord they're playful agents of discord whereas the Horseman is a terrifying beast – an unstoppable machine who does unspeakable things (that must not be spoken of) – so the Expediter – finding out about the Horseman @ the beginning of the story will work to keep him from entering the scene ~&~ since @ the beginning we find out that there's a fly in the ointment – i.e. something's gone wrong – or not quite right – w/ the wall (although Big Bang the universe just always was ~&~ the reason the universe keeps expanding is b/c it's always been expanding although it retains the same exact shape doing so by adding a little bit of matter when needed (which violates the Law of the Conservation of Mass) – then moving on to the Quasi-Steady State Theory wherein the universe continues to expand by a constant series of mini-Big Bangs which create the matter needed for the universe to retain the same look its always had – then moving on to the Big Crunch (or the gnaB giB) which states that the universe will one day stop expanding instead it will contract back down to what it was before the Big Bang ever occurred – moving on to the Big wall that's intended to keep people out should be this wall is more like a piece of modern art that's making a comment on something although the artists (cf. artisans) in question will certainly have no high minded artistic ideas that they wish to convey (unlike w/ the model which is so accurate it might as well be the city itself) so the message will be conveyed in spite of the artists not b/c of them – but the reason the KnoxVillains continue to add on to the city is to cause this very same sort of mayhem (so they are winning) knowing that when the wall is completed they will be thrown out unless the entire scenario is a trick being played by the KnoxVillains then what that may be ~&~ how far along the wall is at this juncture will be unknown) – well the Expediter (for some reason) sends out the Arachnid to take care of this fly (whoever or whatever it may be) – but then it's discovered that there might not be a fly in the ointment – that maybe the KnoxVillains have merely planted this idea into the Expediter's assistant's head (the assistant merely being called "the Assistant") so the Expediter would get machinations going that don't need to be going – hence causing more chaos – if the Arachnid continues on w/ her job to infiltrate a KnoxVillain sect so the Expediter then needs to find a way Bounce (or Oscillating Universe Theory) where the universe expands ~&~ contracts w/in an infinite loop of Big Bangs ~&~ Big Crunches here ignoring the 2nd Law of Thermodynamics b/c such a system would still be closed ~&~ would ∴ run out of energy someday – then on to the Heat Death of the Universe which he will explain does not mean that the universe will burn up instead it will involve that 2nd Law of Thermodynamics b/c the universe being a closed system will someday reach a point where all of the stars will burn out all of the energy will be evenly dispersed thru-out the universe evidenced by a uniform temperature meaning there can no longer be heat transfer ~&~ w/o heat transfer there is they are doubly winning b/c the group has forced even more absurdity (read: entropy) on the city which is a good piece of evidence for the interpretation that says the KnoxVillains were the ones to put up the speakers in the 1st place – were the ones to speak into the sacred microphone through the speakers – were the ones who broadcasted the static ~&~ if you think it was difficult to communicate in Knoxville before what w/ the various dialects – now it's just about impossible since no one can hear anyone else ~&~ the static itself has begun driving people insane but no one will stop the speakers b/c of the possibility of to extract the Arachnid w/o her cover being blown – so it is decided to send out the Blue Jay in order to retrieve the Arachnid who is in search of the fly (for some reason) – but then it is rumored that the Arachnid was originally a double agent somehow connected to whoever was the fly in the ointment so maybe now the Blue Jay is in danger so Felix Feline is sent in to nab the Blue Jay before the Blue Jay makes contact w/ the Arachnid who (it seems) shouldn't have been sent out in the 1st place after the fly – but then it's discovered that the Arachnid's not a double agent instead a triple agent working for the gov. pretending to double cross the no work – ~&~ finally he will come to the Cold Death of the Universe but he doesn't want to talk about the Cold Death something about it bothers him something about it scares him but he won't say what …

| hearing from the Mayor although no one can reach the Mayor ~&~ no one knows just who the Mayor is (still) … | gov. for the KnoxVillains while actually double crossing the double cross ∴ working for the gov. again which might be a quadruple cross (b/c it's entirely too confusing to follow ~&~ ∴ smacks of a KnoxVillain ploy) – so the Expediter decides to cancel the whole thing – doing so by calling in the Old Dawg but then the Assistant informs the Expediter that the Old Dawg can't be contacted – he's missing – so now the Expediter gets the idea that maybe the Arachnid has outed some of the gov.'s agents (although why he sent the Arachnid in in the 1st place is completely unknown) ~&~ w/o any other recourse the Expediter calls in Capricorn to find the Old Dawg who | |

was going to nab Felix Feline who's in search of the Blue Jay who's desperately trying to save the Arachnid who was sent in to take care of the fly (for some reason) although no one's entirely sure why since no one really knows Capricorn – the Assistant merely throws out the name as a possibility ~&~ w/o any other agent to turn to ~&~ although he's a relative unknown freelance agent – Capricorn's called in – but b/c of Capricorn's shady background no one remains content for long ~&~ then the rest of the agents are called into question b/c agents themselves – even good agents – are in the biz for the intrigue ~&~ ∴ liable to join any side that might be interesting – so w/o so much as a shred of real evidence against the Arachnid or Blue Jay or Felix Feline or Old Dawg or Capricorn ~&~ w/o even knowing who the fly in the ointment may be (only speculating that it has something to do w/ the construction of the wall) the Expediter sends in Beau Vine to sort the entire mess out – but then he realizes he doesn't know how to contact Mr. Vine but it doesn't matter b/c the Assistant one day tells the Expediter that Mr. Vine is on the case – but by this time the Expediter's lost all hope in the entire ordeal (thinking: "There was an old woman who swallowed a fly / I don't know why she swallowed a fly / Perhaps she'll die" well he thinks that's an adequate assessment of the system that he may or may not be involved in) – ~&~ he figures even he – the Expediter – could be working for the KnoxVillains w/o realizing it at this stage so he furthermore figures there's no stopping the coming of the Horseman – so he steps out of the office to take a walk in what he thinks is a driving rainstorm except outside it's not raining at all…

… ~&~ I've also decided that the entire story will be written w/o capital letters or quotation marks or breaks for paragraphs ~&~ instead of periods I'll use three spaces ~&~ instead of commas I'll use two spaces – so the entire story will be a block of text only broken by the macro ~&~ micro section breaks ~&~ all of these sections will be montaged together but never

Beginning – Middle – End until the very last macro of the story – forming bursts of metaphors always undercutting what you thought I was going to undercut @ every turn ~&~ then undercutting that undercutment in ~&~ of itself ~&~ I can see in your eye before the look is even there that my thinking about this project has gotten out of control but cf. Kafka where the high command has always existed ~&~ ditto on the plan for the Great Wall – well the direction this is going in was always the direction it was going to go in cf. Borges who cites Baruch Spinoza's "All things long to persist in their being" ~&~ much as Shih Huang Ti "forbade that death be mentioned ~&~ sought the elixir of immortality" – well since this was always the direction it just wants to keep going on – but I can tell you don't want to talk about Kafka or Borges but about Braess ~&~ how extra capacity sometimes lowers performance like when you're in a traffic jam ~&~ you think it'd be better to just cut over to a different road but then everyone follows you ~&~ then there you are in another traffic jam but I don't have time to think about Braess right now or even when you get around to telling me about him b/c anymore all I can do is think about this story – everything else has fallen out of sight although I still can't see that point where the ellipsis will come will leave you hanging but in a way that will have you thinking about your relationship w/ the universe – I still can't see the point where I'll write those famous final two words: THE ... WHAT ...?! ~&~ it's so cold. Freezing. B/c I accidentally tore the adjuster off the thermostat. ~&~ as the white noise increases – it keeps getting colder ...

The Big Bounce (or the Oscillating Universe Theory)

Pretending you understand will not help, obsession w/ the "immense ... gross ... useless" past will not help, so we will face, embrace, <&> erase our fears of the hereafter, our fears of nearing the end, for self-actualization must be our goal, <&> we will hold hands <&> be like a cloud of atoms, each of us indistinguishable from the other, our inner power shining through b/c we cannot let the negative energy of a possibly unhappy conclusion derail us from who we are, we must continue chugging forward, a train of life whose cars are interconnected, whose links hold firm, much as the story will hold firm when it is (<&> it will be) funneled through the Expediter; for you see, the narrator for the 1st macro section will be an intelligent teenager full of ennui (as so many teenagers are who have not sought out their inner calm), <&> the 2nd macro section will be narrated by a confident intellectual (one who still needs to accept the spiritual power of the world), the 3rd by a less confident intellectual, <&> on <&> on just like the description of our friend the Expediter, so the diverse word communities that make up the story will be narrated by a being that sounds like that good soul the main character, so, like an exalted spirit, he will subsume the story, then one whole slice of the tale will be about our friend the Expediter, then the good soul's story (w/ Arachnid, Blue Jay, Felix Feline, Old Dawg, Capricorn, Beau Vine, <&> the Horseman) will unite w/ the rest, the totality, b/c it will be revealed, like a mystical secret w/held for a spiritual purpose, that the Expediter's true name is Musca, the scientific term for "fly," meaning (alas) that our friend Mr. Musca was the fly in the ointment (deep breaths, do not panic), yet this knowledge will not be bestowed upon us until the end, for the Expediter's story shall be told backwards (again, a mystical secret to be only understood thru self-actualization), <&> @ the end (or the beginning for our friend) we will discover that he speaks into an aged golden microphone inscribed w/ the letters "SPQR" that does not appear to be connected to a life-force of its own (no electricity), but the transcendent POV will be that it is ethereally connected to the speakers in Knoxville, that whoever arranged the speakers (as you did in the model) had not reached tranquility, <&> so our unfortunate brother discarded the sacred instrument in a random location, disrupting its balance, causing the static (signaling him as a KnoxVillain), <&> so our friend the Expediter, who comprehends the need for spiritual <&> physical equilibrium, has been the qi-force behind the organization of Knoxville, although unknowingly or perhaps in a transcendent sphere, metaphorically, for the city is an essence mirror which reflects Mr. Musca's views on life, the failed union w/ his spouse, the intellectual ideas that bring no peace, the chaos inside (<&> outside in Knoxville), but he feels w/ each transmission thru the microphone that he <&> the city move as one, hand in hand, toward self-actualization, unless the city is an inner metaphor alone; <&> if the city is an inner metaphor, then when the people, once more, encounter the downtown area, still an orderly grid, <&> they begin taking walks there, thinking that someday their entire city <&> their lives will reach this level of tranquility, for much as our consciousness expands beyond its bounds to the frightening realms of chaos, it too contracts back to its inner peace, then we can take this moment as a symbol for the union of all our souls <&> for our own personal lives (much as Brother Borges tells us we can take the wall as a metaphor, the wall that protects that immense gross useless past); <&> even though the KnoxVillains may continue w/ their plans to unseat our knight named Sir Qi, the Mayor, our master of balance, will air TV commercials that depict the lives of the calm, <&> we will ignore <&> erase from our memories the guerilla broadcasts from the KnoxVillains that falsely claim that uniformity is also a form of entropy, their argument being that if the pistons <&> the cylinders of your car were uniform

then your car would go nowhere; relax; breathe deeply; do not fear the words of the KnoxVillains for they will fall on deaf ears b/c nothing can be heard @ this point, for the only sound that can be taken in is:
shshshshshshshshshshshshshshshshshshshshshshshshsh
shshshshshshshshshshshshshshshshshshshshshshshshsh
shshshshshshshshshshshshshshshshshshshshshshshshsh
shshshshshshshshshshshshshshshshshshshshshshshshsh
shshshshshshshshshshshshshshshshshshshshshshshshsh
shshshshshshshshshshshshshsshshshshshshshshshshshs
hshshshshshshshshshshshshshshshshshshshshshshshshs
hshshshsshshshshshshshshshshshshshshshshshshshshsh
shshshshshshshshshshshshshshshshshshshshshshshshsh
shshshshshshshshshshshshshshshshshshshshshshshshsh
shshshshshshshshshshshshshshshshshshshshshshshshsh
shshshshshshshshshshshshshshshshshshshshshshshshsh
shshshshshshshshshshshshshshshshshshshshshshshshsh
sshshshshshshshshshshshshshshshshshshshshshshshshs
hshshshshshshshshshshshshshshshshshshshshshshshshs
hshshshshshshshshshshshshshshshshshshshshshshshshs
hshshshshshshshshshshshshshshshshshshshshshshshshs
hshshshshshshshshshshshshshshshshshshshshshshshshs
hshshshshshshshshshshshshshshshshshshshshsshshshsh
shshshshshshshshshshshshshshshshshshshshshshshshsh
shshshshshshshshshshshshshshshshshshshshshshshshsh

shshshshshshshshshshshshshshshshshshshshshshshshsh
shshshshshshshshshshshshshshshshshshshshshshshshsh
shshshshshshshshshshshshshshshshshshshshshshshshsh
shshshshshshshshshshshshshshshshsshshshshshshshshs
hshshshshshshshshshshshshshshshshshshshshshshshshs
hshshshshshshshshshshshshshshshshshshshshshshshshs
hshshshshshshshshshshshshshshshshshshshshshshshshs
hshshshshshshshshshshshshshshshshshshshshshshshshs
hshshshshshshshshshshshshshshshshshshshshshshshshs
hshshshshshshshshshshshsshshshshshshshshshshshshsh
shshshshshshshshshshshshshshshshshshshshshshshshsh
shshshshshshshshshshshshshshshshshshshshshshshshsh
shshshshshshshshshshshshshshshshshshshshshshshshsh
shshshshshshshshshshshshshshshshshshshshshshshshsh
shshhshshshshshshshshshshshshshshshshshshshshshshs
hshshshshshshshshshsshshshshshshshshshshshshshshsh
shshshshshshshshshshshshshshshshshshshshshshshshsh
shshshshshshshshshshshshshshshshshshshshshshshshsh
shshshshshshshshshshshshshshshshshshshshshshshshsh
shshshshshshshshshshshshshshshshshshshshshshshshsh

b/c the speakers (sabotaged by the KnoxVillains) have lost their true connection, <&>, yes, there have been good souls sent away from this earth b/c our friends have not retained their inner calm <&> have allowed the static to disrupt their qi, but remember, there's still the Mayor, the Mayor will bring about order, will make life worth living, <&> the Mayor might be our friend the Expediter, or the being the Expediter could be when he has attained self-actualization, but for now meditate on the Knoxville that will arise once the wall is completed, <&> do not think that your grand architectural plans will set you drifting into hopelessness, recall that Brother Kafka has advised you to rejoice in your usefulness to the construction (of the wall of the story)—it could not be done w/o you; <&> then, also recall that the Expediter will one day be a physics professor, searching for balance by contemplating the grand conclusion, <&> the homilies on the various theories will be tapes made by that good soul Mr. Musca, recorded during his time as the Expediter, <&> this will be the final loose end that will be wrapped up to complete the unification process, meaning the story itself will reach its own inner peace in the main character, who will come to understand the Great Passage:

> [1]There was an old woman who
> swallowed a fly,
> [2]I don't know why she
> swallowed a fly,
> [3]Perhaps she'll die,

where the old woman is the Old Knoxville, the Chaotic Knoxville that will pass away when the pacifying power of the Expediter is visited upon it; <&> you will *pretend* to be relieved, having not reached self-actualization quite yet, by the fact that the story comes down to *a* character, that the other sections are all contained in him, a spiritual vessel; you will pretend to be, but you will not *be* relieved; <&> so you will try to ignore, instead of facing, the KnoxVillain-like notion that if the tale is contained in one person, then the story is a closed system, <&> closed systems (e.g., the universe) are subject to entropy (relax, deep breaths), <&> you will *pretend* to not reflect on the fact that the Sunsphere, a microphone itself once, is now deconstructed <&> part of a ziggurat; you will instead *pretend* that you have attained tranquility, that you have already self-actualized, that you are prepared for whatever end that may transpire in the hereafter, but you are not. Much as the ice has thrown off my own balance. So cold. So cold.

The Big Crunch (or gnaB giB)

FYI, you will believe that it's over, in … the … future …, when you encounter the story, the ideas to the story, right now maybe you have an inkling, maybe not even that much, my twin, but in … the … future …, when you hear about this piece, when we go thru all that we will have gone thru together, w/ you even building a model to give yourself something to look @ in relation to this story! when we reach this point, you will believe it's over, it couldn't possibly expand any further, who wants it to expand any further? not me, not you, not even Kafka or Borges, this turgidity couldn't possibly continue, so it has to be … but it won't be, for now we must get to the essence of the tale, >&, much as you believe expansion, at this stage, is impossible, there's no more outward momentum, we must now move inward to deal w/ the … pages … >& pages of notes (oh so many), but I can no longer see this as a story, as any coherent story, it's become a novella, a novel, a series of novels, an encyclopedia all itself, so much as Shih Huang Ti demanded that all books written before his reign must be burned, demanded that he be called The First in order to be the first person ever, called himself Huang Ti "the legendary emperor who invented writing >& the compass," hence bringing everything back to the point of the commencement, I have decided not to write *this* … story, instead I will replace it w/ a story about writing this … story, using the story itself as a metaphor for entropy >& the end of the universe, knowing what you will think, allowing you to become the main character, to subsume the Expediter who subsumed the entire … story, ∴ , I allow you to subsume the story; I have (or will have) waited too long for Kafka's courier from the Imperial Palace to deliver the emperor's message that says, in no uncertain terms, just how to step outside this work >& see it whole, which would then enable me to give it a true form, a true function that you would be proud of in … the … future, I can only see it as an ever-expanding … story, formless, shapeless, but we need order, we must get back to *that* singularity, which is what the people of Knoxville, improbably, have done, or are, at least, On The Verge of Doing, for the Knoxvillians have almost completed their wall, >& already people are being banished as members of KnoxVillain sects (or who are under suspicion of being KnoxVillains), but as the banishments are enacted, it will be found that an innocent person was accidentally put on one of the expulsion lists (absurd b/c so many innocent people will be banished), >& that is the problem the Expediter's been dealing w/ thru-out, only in reverse, >& now that person must be found amongst the KnoxVillain hordes outside the mostly completed wall, but as we already know, after the entire ordeal, the Expediter doesn't want to be an expediter anymore, >& just as he's walking off the job (into his ... future of being a physics professor who focuses on the end of the universe), the gates ... open to readmit the innocent man, >& the innocent man enters Knoxville, >& makes an appearance next to the ziggurat Sunsphere, riding a horse, >& the static will finally cease, so although everything will appear to be fine, w/ the wall almost finished >& the city well on its way back to the 1950s >& a possible reconnection w/ the Mayor about to be established (at least, that's what the people think), someone who appears to be the Horseman will return, >& then we will remember from the 1st (>& ∴ the last) scene w/ the Expediter, that he doesn't care, that it doesn't bother him in the least that the Horseman may be coming into the city b/c he's accepted it, he's become the reflection of the children's song There ... was an old wo.man who swal.lowed a fly ... I don't know why ... she swal..lowed a fly ... Per ... haps she'll ... die ... which doesn't exactly sound like we're supposed to ... fear for the woman, but that instead it's merely a fact of life, that after one absurdity, another absurdity may arise, the final absurdity, or maybe there'll be an entire list of absurdities involving spiders, birds, cats, dogs, goats, cows, >& horses, >& that maybe ..., maybe even after all of that ... absurdity, the absurdity to end all absurdities will still occur, which is what you will believe there in ... the ... future ..., what you will believe before I decide to make the move to the nth absurdity >& transform this into a story about a story, about you, my twin; but really, you aren't my twin, we are more like Theseus' ship: you are made of replacement parts, perhaps inferior replacement parts, there in ... the ...future. >& I don't even mind the chill in my apartment anymore. I've grown used to the cold.

The Cold Death of the Universe

You will want it to stop. But it won't stop, even if it is your story, it will continue on forever, w/ or w/o you, there will be stacks of paper to the ceiling, blocking the door, heaped on the furniture, but still it will go on no matter how disgusting for you, for you are Shih Huang Ti (what character or person or being isn't?) b/c no matter how much evidence you are given to the contrary, you still think you're the center of the universe, though it doesn't bother you that the universe, the story may stop someday, it's abhorrent to think its purpose might include you so little it would abandon your very existence to keep expanding, that you'll be used like propellant to keep the whole thing going, but try w/ all your might to comprehend the universe, the story, but only up to a certain point, then avoid further meditation (Kafka) b/c all arts aspire to the state of music, which is pure form (Borges) ... you find yourself in your model, or in Knoxville, for they are the same, standing right next to the ziggurat Sunsphere, the Sunsphere will begin moving until it can't be seen anymore, the temperature will drop lower, lower, you'll want it to stop, to cease, to remain sort of stable, no – to remain stable, hell, to go to pieces, to bounce backforth btw coherence/incoherence w/in a finite span, to revert to an ∞ly dense dot, anything, anything but this ∞ expansion, but nobody cares what *you* want, nothing cares what *you* want—

> There was an etc. who etc.
> I don't know why etc.
> Perhaps etc. etc.

the pages continue w/o any sign of termination, soon not only will the Sunsphere be out of sight, but the sky will darken, the stars all dying, but the story, the universe goes on, not a single line expurgated, all of the energy available used for one purpose: expansion, then, all by yourself, in a timeless zone, the center of nothing, you understand that although there will be no one to read it, the story'll just keep going on,

>There was etc. etc.
>I don't know etc.
>Perhaps etc. etc. etc …

because there are plenty more ideas, oh the ideas, the ideas, the ideas, *AND!* although you will, the universe, the story will never come to an

You Are Where I Am Not

I am not a real person. I am only words on paper. A narrator. A narrator of the first-person variety. An invention. A fake. Or, if you prefer, an illusion. And yet, if I tell you there is a city, you will see a city. And yet, if I tell you that I walk through a ruined city, you will see a ruined city and you will see me walking through it. You will see a ruined city and you will tell yourself that you're there and you're seeing it through my eyes. Through the eyes of the narrator. Through me. Though there is no me. I do not exist. I am only words. *I am a narrator.*

The city was destroyed some time ago. It was destroyed by an explosion. An explosion from above. It could have been a bomb, or a missile, or even an event like the Tunguska, the Cando, the Vitim, or the Eastern Mediterranean. From atop a ruined skyscraper I can see that the blast pattern is in the shape of a butterfly. I can see that the blast pattern is in the shape of a Comma butterfly from the family *Nymphalidae*. Although the shape is perfect, the coloring is not quite right being rust red and gray and black and brown. I can see that the trees in the park at the center of the city have been stripped but remain as superfluous telephone poles, whereas the trees in the wings of the Comma have been knocked over. The airburst object entered at thirty degrees. There was no warning. There was no escape.

But I was not here when the city was destroyed. I was not here when it was destroyed, though I was also not somewhere else, anywhere else; I was nowhere else, nowhere to be found, nowhere. I did not yet exist when the city was struck by the event, and I still do not exist in this city that has been in its post-event stage for some time. The weeds peek through the rubble, and the rats and cockroaches are everywhere. Roads here are made of detritus as if the building materials for all the past and future boulevards existed at the same time, ready for trans-dimensional beings to construct hyperspace thoroughfares through the multiverse, intersecting with other hyperspace thoroughfares, taking you wherever you want to go, showing you whatever you want to see.

As I walk through, as I ascend structures that may collapse under my negligible weight, as I sit on park benches now located in the middle of dry fountains, as I board streetcars bound for no destination, as I converse with ashen silhouettes of former shadows of the previous inhabitants of this municipality, as I take my seat in theaters that lack stages (unless the wreckage across the street can now be called a stage), and as I sleep in woefully overrated five star hotels I begin to think that this city could rise again. It could, in fact, follow the same pattern it followed during its original development, from an outpost, to a settlement, to a small manufacturing town, to a large industrial city, to an industrial and commercial metropolis, to a post-industrial megalopolis; it could be known for steel, glass, rubber, meat, textiles, investment banking, computers, social services, art, or any combination of these, including other such possibilities absent from this list. I cannot tell you. I would tell you more, but ...

But I have never lived here. I do not live here now. I never knew this city when it was an actual city. I know it merely as a shell. It might've always been like this. The supposed former megalopolis I walk through could be a massive art installation. It could be a massive art installation called *The Fallen Leaf* or *Polygonia c-album*, the Latin name for the Comma butterfly. It's possible that there never was a time when this city was anything but what it currently is: a ruin built to resemble an urban area affected by a Tunguska-like event. The ruin may have been constructed for some dubious reason, and now you believe me complicit in the ruse that's been enacted, you believe that I am in the confidence racket, a charlatan who has pulled you in.

However, much as the city may be an art installation, it may be anything else; it might even not be that one thing you wish it wasn't. I would tell you more about the city, yet not only have I never lived there, I have never been. To me it does not exist, since I do not exist. I do not exist because I am only words on paper. Yet as I stroll along the roads connecting one dimension to the next, I notice that whereas I am neither there nor elsewhere, in some dimensions *you* are there, perhaps not fully trusting me, secretly blaming me for your uncertainty, wondering what to do with me, wondering what to do with the hoard of airborne Comma butterflies, wondering what to do with the falling leaves, wondering what to make of this city, wondering what happened to it, if anything, wondering what will come of it, unsure, as if you could not trust your senses, as if you were looking through someone else's eyes, as if you were looking through my eyes, the eyes of the first person variety narrator, though I am an invention, a fake, an illusion, though *I* am just not there.

Photo: Jacob Knabb

Andrew Farkas is the author of two short fiction collections: *Sunsphere* (BlazeVOX Books) and *Self-Titled Debut* (Subito Press), and a novel: *The Big Red Herring* (KERNPUNKT Press). His work has appeared in *The Iowa Review*, *North American Review*, *The Cincinnati Review*, *The Florida Review*, *Western Humanities Review*, *Denver Quarterly*, and elsewhere. He has been thrice nominated for a Pushcart Prize, including one Special Mention in *Pushcart Prize XXXV* and one Notable Essay in *Best American Essays 2013*. He holds a Ph.D. from the University of Illinois at Chicago, an M.F.A. from the University of Alabama, an M.A. from the University of Tennessee, and a B.A. from Kent State University. He is a fiction editor for *The Collagist* and an Assistant Professor of English at Washburn University. He lives in Lawrence, Kansas.

Made in the USA
Columbia, SC
09 September 2024